Praise for *The Liminal People*

"The action sequences are smartly orchestrated, but it is Taggert's quest to retrieve his own soul that gives *The Liminal People* its oomph. Jama-Everett has done a stellar job of creating a setup that promises even greater rewards in future volumes." [San Francisco Chronicle]

"For all the grit, character and poetry on display here, Everett's own super power appears to be plotting and set-pieces. Readers will find a quick immersion in the opening scene, and then some secret world-building. Once the plot kicks in, readers had best be prepared to finish the book in one sitting, while experiencing better special effects than you will find in any movie. Indeed, Everett's prose is cinematic in the best sense; when he puts us in a scene of action, his descriptions take on a hyper-clarity that is better than telepathy. The plot arc is cunning and enjoyably surprising, and the revelations have the shock of the new but the old-school satisfaction of well-woven espionage plots. *The Liminal People* is seriously well-written, but also seriously fun to read. It's a secret world that deserves the elegant exposition of this engaging novel—and a sequel, sooner rather than later." [Rick Kleffel, The Agony Column]

"The story's setup . . . takes next to no time to relate in Jama-Everett's brisk prose. With flat-voiced, sharp-edged humor reminiscent of the razors his fellow thugs wear around their necks, Taggert claims to read bodies 'the way pretentious East Coast Americans read *The New Yorker* . . . I've got skills,' he adds. 'What I don't have is patience.'" [Nisi Shawl, The Seattle Times]

"Every once in awhile, a first novel catches you by surprise. Sometimes it's the style and sometimes it's the pure originality or unique mixing of influences. In the case of Ayize Jama-Everett's *The Liminal People*, the pleasure comes from all of the above." [Jeff VanderMeer, Omnivoracious]

"Ayize Jama-Everett has brewed a voodoo cauldron of Sci-Fi, Romance, Crime, and Superhero Comic, to provide us with a true gestalt of understanding, offering us both a new definition of "family" and a world view on the universality of human conduct. *The Liminal People*—as obviously intended—will draw different reactions from different readers. But none of them will stop reading until its cataclysmic ending." [Andrew Vachss]

"Ayize's imagination will mess with yours, and the world won't ever look quite the same again." [Nalo Hopkinson]

"*The Liminal People* has the pleasures of classic sf while being astonishingly contemporary and savvy." [Maureen F. McHugh]

"Fast and sleek and powerful—a skillful and unique mix of supernatural adventure and lived-in, persuasive, often moving noir." [Felix Gilman]

"An astounding first novel. . . . *The Liminal People* is a noir juggernaut with startlingly genuine themes of salvation, emancipation, and family. As of now, this book is my favorite of the year and I desperately hope that Jama-Everett chooses to pen a sequel." [Elitist Book Reviews]

"Fast-paced and frequently violent, Jama-Everett's engaging and fulfilling debut offers a compelling take on the classic science-fiction convention of the powerful misfit; incorporates an interesting, multiethnic cast of characters; and proves successful as both an action-packed thriller and a careful look at the moral dilemmas of those whose powers transcend humanity."
[Publishers Weekly]

"Razor. Plush. Fast." [Tan, City Lights Books, San Francisco, CA]

"Compact but creative, and filled with good ideas and elements of classic sci-fi, noir, and superhero stories." [Peter, Brookline Booksmith, Brookline, MA]

"From within 'The Golden Ghetto' Jama-Everett has created a book that resists classification, joining the Afrosurreal Pantheon of writers exploring this new-found freedom. He calls the gifted ones Liminal People, people 'Always on the borderland, the threshold, the in-between.' He has Taggert explain. 'I learned what I know by walking the liminal lands.' I trust that many people will relate, or will want to." [D. Scot Miller, City Lights Blog]

THE
LIMINAL
WAR

THE LIMINAL WAR

AYIZE JAMA-EVERETT

Small Beer Press
Easthampton, MA

The Liminal War copyright © 2015 by Ayize Jama-Everett. All rights reserved.
liminaleob.tumblr.com

Small Beer Press
150 Pleasant Street, #306
Easthampton, MA 01027
smallbeerpress.com
weightlessbooks.com
info@smallbeerpress.com

Distributed to the trade by Consortium.

Library of Congress Cataloging-in-Publication Data

Jama-Everett, Ayize, 1974-
  The liminal war / Ayize Jama-Everett.
      pages cm
  Summary: "Taggert wants to look after his family so when his adopted daughter disappears he
only has one option: find her"-- Provided by publisher.
  ISBN 978-1-61873-101-2 (paperback) -- ISBN 978-1-61873-102-9 (ebook)
  1. Healers--Fiction. 2. Extrasensory perception--Fiction. 3. Missing persons--Fiction. 4. Psy-
chological fiction. 5. Suspense fiction. I. Title.
  PS3610.A426L57 2015
  813'.6--dc23
                                    2015010349

First edition 1 2 3 4 5 6 7 8 9

Text set in Minion 12 pt.

This book was printed on 30% PCW recycled paper by the Maple Press in York, PA.
Cover illustration by John Jennings (jijennin70.tumblr.com).

For Nia.

ACT I

London, fourteen minutes from now

Chapter One

"They say you can cure my cancer."

"Who is 'they'?" It's a genuine question. Lots of people talk about me.

"People that I trust."

She's old, white, manicured, and comes from a titled family. I shouldn't be in the same room with her, even with this false East Indian face and body on. She's nothing but attention. But the location is anonymous enough—a two-room lightly furnished office paid for in cash, in the heart of Metro London—that I risk her continued, dignified begging.

"That does me no good. Give me a name or I walk."

"I will not betray the people that have gotten me this far with you." A little backbone. I like it. Not like I'll let her know.

"And how do I know those who mean to do me harm haven't sent you?"

"I get the sense you don't suffer your enemies to live for very long."

"So long as that's clear."

✳

I read bodies the way master musicians read music. The closer I get, the more I can see and the more I can influence, change, heal . . . or hurt. I spent years hurting—others, and myself—for a shadow of a pestilence named Nordeen. Head of a team of murder-oriented smugglers called the Razor Neck crew, Nordeen was part father, part slavemaster, all boss. Three years ago I paid for my freedom and family with the life of the only woman I'd ever truly loved: Yasmine. Since then I've been keeping a low profile with our daughter, Tamara, and another liminal teenager in need named Prentis.

It was Samantha's idea to get into healing. No fixed location, no flat fee, no credit cards. Just put a whisper into the no-hope cancer streams, in terminal AIDS wards, among the undiagnosed critical patients, and see who comes.

"But why?" I asked Samantha after she brought it up for the fifth time.

"You have years of practice as a dealer of destruction. Why not aim toward health?" Sam has that way of making me feel like an idiot with simple statements.

The Dame with a backbone has a pernicious brain cancer. Last night I read her from a distance. Rather, I read the chromosomal signature of the cancer. I haven't seen it before, but I've met its cousins and uncles in my other patients. The woman is not nearly as interesting as her disease.

"Breathe easy and try not to move," I tell the Dame, and go deep. Starving out the tendrils drifting into her spine and lungs is easy. I run an experimental serotonin/dopamine blend through her as I block all neural pain pathways. She relaxes instantly. All that's left is the golf-ball-sized toxic cluster of spastic nerve spindles and fibrous tissue in her cerebellum. I deaden its noxious abilities instantly; reducing it will take more time and focus so that the surrounding tissue doesn't overcompensate or remain regressed as a result of the pressure the tumor has put on it. I could beat the tumor back, get the Dame's body to send a sustained electric pulse into the heart of that dead tumor star. But I want to comprehend the beast, figure out why it grew there as opposed to in her hippocampus, or liver for that matter. Sam was right. This has turned into fun for me.

But the Dame starts panicking. Not an indigenous panic either. Someone else, another person like me, a Liminal, is pushing the Dame's fight or flight buttons like she was a stuck elevator. I know because the same thing is happening to me.

A heroin-sized high is enough to knock the Dame unconscious. I turn my ability inward and reduce my doubling hippocampus as it reacts to the fear. I'm calm just in time to hear cars crash right in front of the Tate Modern. At the window I confirm what I've feared. Half of London is in a full-blown panic. Whatever did this—it's not targeted.

Liminals—folks like myself, born with a variety of abilities and skills—tend to be . . . difficult. With no template of appropriate behavior, a Liminal with the ability to enter dreams can be a fairy godmother or a psychic rapist. My brother, with hard telekinetic abilities, chose the latter route. But this is different. There is no maliciousness in this psychic hijack. In fact, this is no attack: this is terror shared.

I hit Holland Street, heading away from the Thames in default healing mode. If I can't reset the panic centers in any of the growing crowds in under two seconds, I just knock them out. I've seen something like this before: 2007, Kuala Lumpur, Mont Kiara. I want to handle this the way I handled that: track the Liminal based off of the victims' symptoms. The closest to the Liminal will be the most severely affected. If I were still with Nordeen, I'd find the Liminal and either me or one of the Razor Neck crew—his pack of murder oriented smugglers—would deal the death. But there's something familiar about this Liminal.

"Prentis," I call out. Usually an animal of some sort—a dog or a mouse—will donate its attention to me if she can hear through them. Prentis is a liminal animal totem; a conduit for animals, but the link works both ways. She knows every move every animal in London makes. But as I dodge a Mini Cooper hopping up the curb, all I get is a flock of pigeons. I follow the progressively more severe fear symptoms over to Trafalgar Square before I reach out with my mind to Tamara.

"Kid, you getting this?" I can't call Tamara my daughter to her face, and given that she's one of the strongest telepaths I've ever met, I've got to be careful not to think it too much either. When her mom Yasmine, realized she was pregnant, she kicked me out without letting me know about our girl. Tamara grew up calling a progressive politician in the Reform Labor Party daddy. When the car Tamara's parents and I were in blew up, she blamed me for their deaths and threw me out a plate-glass window. For a while I thought I deserved it.

Then it hits me. This type of panic has Tamara written all over it. She's usually a sarcastic, semi-streetwise, crafty git. But when she gets truly scared, all that bravado and control disappears. For whatever reason, she's infected every man, woman, and child near her with a mind-crushing panic. The streets are flooded with people crying, breaking down, and hiding. Traffic is worse than usual, with every other driver paranoid about turning the wheel. This ends soon or a lot of people die.

"Tamara, can you feel me? You've got to calm down." I think hard. It's harder for her to not sense my thoughts than to include them. What little I can feel from her feels like she's subsumed. Whatever this is, it's not intentional. Not that it'll matter if she drives everyone nuts.

I kill all lactic acid production in my body, super myelinate my leg muscles, and triple my lung efficiency as I start running. It's a more public display of my skills than I like—including dropping my North Indian face and skeletal structure—but I don't have a lot of time. Nordeen has a vicious dislike for public displays of power. In another life he'd have sent me to handle an outbreak like this: I'd rather not meet my replacement right now.

The closer I get to Tamara's radiating panic, the more twisted metal and screams take over the streets. I want to walk Sam's path and heal everyone around me, but I'd be exhausted and useless by the time I got to my girl. My old path would leave a trail of dead bodies behind me. Instead, I compromise; healing those with heart conditions and knocking out the rest with prodigious opioid flushes to the brain. But as I discharge my power I feel one area of calm. As London Town loses its collective shit, tranquility and ease radiate from Eel Pie Island, some ten-plus miles away from me. It's a steady and progressive calm, chilling people out in a far more gentle way than I could. If I didn't have to get to Tamara, I'd investigate. But my daughter is losing it. And what's worse, I know she's at the last place she should be.

When a Liminal named Alia—a consummate illusionist—killed Tamara's parents, Tamara got smart and hid in an abandoned tube station that Prentis used to call home. We handled Alia and her ilk, and the girls gave up their "pit of sadness," as I called it. But when I have to heal ten seizing pensioners at the entrance to that very tube station, I know that's where Tam is. I hit the tracks and start running toward it, knowing she's not alone.

Walled behind an impressive stack of cement blocks, the station usually goes unmolested. I enter to the sounds of combat, those huge bricks being hurled and smashed into dust. Tamara is as impressive as ever in her open trench coat, open-finger gloves, Gore-Tex T-shirt, and baggy jeans. Her target is a diminutive, super-dark Indian man with no shoes or shirt. Every sixty-pound block Tam throws at him with her telekinesis, the Indian either dodges or destroys with one blow. Another Liminal.

I reach out to give him the Dame's cancer, but where I should feel a four limbs and a head there is only dense void in the shape of a human body. I'm terrified. This thing was not born; it was made out of cold and absence.

I push past my fear, cut off any receptive senses my healing usually offers, and infect his . . . its . . . "bones" with a rampant marrow infection. That stops his jackrabbit punching moving sessions. Briefly.

"Tam, you okay?" I shout, trying to get closer to her, rounding the semi-dazed Indian like he's a wounded animal.

"She's gone, Tag!" she shouts back, using her mouth and mind.

"Dial it back! You're too loud." And like that, London can calm down again. It's an afterthought for her. "Who's gone?"

"Prentis! We were supposed to meet two hours ago, but she's gone!"

"The healer." Never heard such a voice. It's a restrained maliciousness, a voice to be heard in the dark chill of space. I guess Nordeen's new assassin doesn't care much for me.

"Bring it in, kid." I tell Tam. I haven't just been living with the girls. I've been training them to fight. And, more importantly, to work in concert with each other and me. Personality clashes aside, we fight in unison. Tam takes the cue, pushing her long dark hair aside. I pull butterfly knives from my sleeves, up my reflex muscle coordination, and lock in on the assassin.

"What is he?" Tamara demands, lifting two cement blocks behind the man silently while we all circle each other. As usual, Tam thinks we can handle anything. But this . . . entity just incorporated the bone infection into its body in under ten seconds and seems no worse for wear.

"It ain't liminal . . ." is all I can say before Tam launches the two blocks silently at the back of the Indian's head. He responds with perfect backwards weaves that leave Tam and I avoiding those very same blocks. We're separated, and I launch one knife dead center at the stranger's head.

Vipers can't move as fast as this guy. He catches, turns, and re-launches my blade directly into my sternum in less time than it took me to throw it. Off pure instinct I grow five inches of bone at my solar plexus in the millisecond before it hits me.

"Tag!" Again Tamara with the shouting. Only this time it's directed at the Indian. She should know I'm okay. I heal quick. But the shock of seeing me caught off guard triggered something in her. She's given up on bricks and seized the Indian by the short and curlies. She's literally trying to pull his head off his body, yet somehow he's resisting.

"You don't understand . . . ," he says in a voice so calm I almost believe him.

"Well, your powers of explanation suck." Tam jokes. She feels in control.

"Go easy, kid. He might know about Prentis," I tell her as I pull the butterfly knife from my chest.

She makes a rage-filled rookie telepath mistake and enters the Indian's mind. Whatever pestilence she finds in there fucks her concentration and balance. She drops the Indian and is out of commission. I square up.

"Best thing for you to do right now is tell me where Prentis is then go back to Nordeen and remind him of the kindness he extended to me." The shadow in an Indian body stiffens at Nordeen's name.

"I don't know this Prentis. And Nordeen is not one to extend kindness." The Indian doesn't move on me. Instead he sidesteps back and to the remaining sidewall. From the hole in the cement blocks, a younger guy—black with long dreads, in beige and black casual clubwear—steps into the dilapidated station. I don't know him, but I recognize his smell.

"Narayana." His voice chastises the Indian after he sees Tam. "What did you do?"

"I am the sharp knife the inexperienced cut themselves on."

I scan Tam quickly. Physically she's fine. "If you've done permanent damage, death will be a holiday," I let him know. Right as beige boy tries to speak, Samantha, my Sam, comes through the hole, smelling of her sweet and foreign smoke, the same scent that stranger number two reeks of. Her deep black skin is set off perfectly by her dark purple blouse. She runs to me immediately, wrapping my waist with her arms, her tight cornrows in my face. Part of her ability is a control of pheromones, and, though it rarely works with me, I feel her attempt to flood me with calming doses. Her tight oval face betrays her, though. She's angry.

"Mico, get him out of here. His kind and mine never mix well. I told you!" she says in her slight Ethiopian accent, pointing at the shadow of a thing in the corner: Narayana.

"Tell me you're okay," Sam whispers in my ear.

"I'm fine," I lie. She holds my face in her hands and stares me into believing my own words. "I'm fine."

The Indian disappears without a sound. Beige boy, Mico, is kneeling patiently next to Tamara. I move to intercept him, but Samantha puts a gentle hand right where the blade was, asking me in her own way to wait.

"It's okay, Tamara. You can let it all go. He's gone. You're safe." Mico is sincere . . . and more: his voice holds a chorus of thoughts, a low chattering hum. He scans as human . . . and more. It's that scent. The smoke Samantha venerates.

"You don't know anything," Tamara hisses through tears. "You don't understand. None of you do. Prentis is gone."

"We'll find her," I tell her, squatting with the both of them.

"No, Tag." She grabs hold of me like a drowning woman. "She's not gone from London. She's gone from the planet. I can't find her anywhere. She's disappeared. She's dead."

Chapter Two

Sam co-signed on Mico, claiming she's been meaning to have us meet.
Tam ceded to the retreat despite her long-standing distrust of Samantha. She swears I reek of the Ethiopian every time I come back from hanging with her.

"I did this?" Tamara asked as she surveyed the damage of her psychic tantrum. While the panic was done, the wreckage of people, overturned buses, and destroyed shops was just beginning to come together.

"I didn't mean to . . . ," my girl started.

"I know." I stopped her. "Business time, girl. We deal with the guilt later." Sam noticed my work tone with a distant curiosity but said nothing.

I half thought Mico was going to walk us to Eel Pie Island until a silver town car rounded the corner by Battersea Park—piloted by the Indian. Mico stepped in like he was expecting it to be there all along. Samantha held the door open for us, but Tam stiffened at moving in.

"I give you my word. Narayana won't harm you."

"What good's your word then?" Tam snapped back in her proper London tough accent.

"Not the time," I say, pushing gently past the both of them and getting in the car. Their antipathy is almost biological. Most people conform to Samantha's desires, unconscious of her sway. Tamara's telepathy gives her complete awareness of her psychic state and a latent distrust of any influence. Thankfully, her training kicks in. There'll be time enough for the penny-ante shit once we lay eyes on Prentis.

Whatever Narayana is gets me sick just by looking at him. And I don't get sick. But a little girl I promised to protect, a girl Tam and I both call our heart, is missing. Somehow, despite her shit life, Prentis has managed to hold on to the joy of each moment with a kind of reckless abandon—an abandon I witnessed die in Tamara's eyes the day she sliced Alia in two. That little animal girl shared her joy, her love, with us in a way that made us better, stronger. I focus on her voice, her laugh, her psychotic wardrobe choices as the not-human Indian careens through accidents and open road with the same savage coordination that made him an impossible target in the tube station. We're at the Twickenham Rivers Bridge to Eel Pie Island quicker than we have a right to be. No one speaks the entire ride, though I feel the power and the eyes of two annoyed women on me. Even Mico hides the muscle twitch of a smirk as I sit between them.

"Please stay close to me, Tamara," Mico requests as we're about to exit the car. "Your . . . troubles didn't go unnoticed by our community. Some may still consider you a threat."

"Insightful folks here then, ennit?" my girl snaps.

"More than you know," Mico agrees and exits the car.

Apparently Eel Pie Island used to be rocker central back in the day. Listen to the island residents and they'll bore you with this band and that artist that used to live on the island in the Thames. In the late '90s the seminal hotel on the island burned to the ground, and it's functioned as a refuge for the financially stable artistic since. Mico says it's also a seat of ley lines crossing the Red Dragon's Head, whatever the hell that means.

Those on the street smile when they see Mico, then glare hard when they see Tamara. Narayana stayed with the car, so only Samantha and I tail behind them. From art houses and mixed-up two bedrooms, groups of humans no smaller than five give our crew a cautious twice-over as we make our way to the remains of the burned-out hotel, now being rebuilt. None of them are Liminal or whatever Narayana is, but they are not . . . typical. They're breathing like they're taking turns supplying air to an invisible body. To a one, all their biorhythms are coordinated.

"Floors three and below are perfectly safe," Mico says, leading us through a set of wall-sized double doors to a banquet hall on the first floor. A half-room ebony wood table and elaborate window and door moldings are the only hints at the room's previous ostentatiousness. "We're still working on construction above. I had folks bring some honey wine and fruit. The bathrooms are at the end of the hall. I'd love the opportunity to talk, answer any and all questions, but I need to calm the community down. Might take a few hours."

"Prentis—" Tam starts.

"Thanks for the kindness," I interrupt. "We'll wait here."

"I promise we'll find your friend," Mico says with a sincerity that makes me want to believe. He leaves, and I notice his swagger and American accent.

"Taggert," Sam starts.

"Can we get some alone time?" I ask Sam without turning to look at her.

Mico, Narayana, this island; Samantha's known about all of this and told me nothing. I've had enough with lies and mistrust in my life. I hear the double doors close behind me.

"Skank," Tamara says.

"What happened?"

"Can I show you?" Meaning, can she replay the events in my mind? Between us, and Prentis, we've gone days not speaking, using our powers with and on each other in a more effective form of communication than words could ever be. But right now, I need words.

"Use your words," I snap.

"You mad at me?"

"I'm worried you don't understand what's going on. We're supposed to be laying low, remember? Sight unseen. But you just psychically pimp-slapped all of London. By mistake. Then you launched yourself into the mind of an I-don't-even-know-what. Now you can't even say how you got all wound up."

"I can, it just . . ."

"Hurts. I know, kid. But you run from the hurt it just gets worse. Words force your brain to make meaning. And that's what we need now, meaning."

She nods, breathes deeps, squats to the ground, and then stands again, her eyes only slightly wet. I pull up a large, puffy green upholstered chair, and she does the same.

"We were doing our hide-and-seek practice, you know?" Her first lesson was to hide in plain sight. Tamara taking advantage of people's peripheral blindness, Prentis blending into what she called the primitive musk, the general sense of humanity that lacks definition.

"Was hiding down by the wharf. Going for a challenge given all the rats and gulls, yeah? But I'm so focused on them, the rats, I miss this stray dog just staring at me from one of the ships. So I call it, figuring she got me. So I go public, let all the dogs, rats, birds, everyone see me, yeah? Nothing. So I call and that's when I felt it . . ."

"No connection."

"Not a thing, Tag. I've felt her on one level or another since we all linked up. Even masked, even hiding, there's a Prentis-shaped hole. Same with you. But there was nothing. Looked as best I could through every set of eyes in London . . ."

"Look through eyes here?" I ask.

"Say again?"

"You get any Eel Pie eyes?" She thinks about it then shakes her head, no. "Think she's here?" Tam asks.

"Doubt this bunch would be able to hold her if she didn't want to be held. Plus bringing us here would be dumb." I go silent, so she continues.

"I look best I can through as many eyes as I can. Nothing. I know I should've checked with you first, but I got scared. I listened to the world, every thought, just trying to find mention of her. Nothing. No one. I freaked. I'm sorry that I lost it, but I fucking lost it. I've never felt someone just go like that. Not even Mom . . . I didn't realize I was projecting. I just went to the place I knew she'd go if there was a problem. I was there maybe ten minutes before that—what was that guy?—came."

"She seeing anyone?" I ask.

"What? Like, shagging? Piss off."

"New friends? Old enemies?"

"We're her only real friends, and you know what happened to her old enemies." Tam pauses, goes to the gigantic red stained-glass windows, and looks out at the Thames. For a second she looks like her mother.

"She dead, Tag?"

"No," I say, standing and going to her. Much as Prentis's disappearance is getting to her, I know where the look of concern comes from, and I won't avoid it. "You never told me you felt your mom's . . . death."

"It wrecked me." She chokes.

"It wasn't the absence," I tell her, standing behind her, bearing witness to the same low-hanging sky going gray. "It was the fading of her . . . self on the mental plane. That can't be replicated. Dead is dead. I don't know what happened to Prentis, but you didn't feel that fade. She's not dead."

It doesn't last long. It's brief, strong and swift: she hugs me. For a few seconds, I feel like a father.

"Right, so who are these hippies then?" Tam viciously massacres all the tears on her light brown face.

"Fucking mystery." I exhale, grabbing a bottle of honey wine, and pour two glasses. "But a synchronized one. The rank and file outside breathe together like a well-coordinated machine. You notice how Mico knew where the car would be?"

"Why don't you ask your girlfriend?" she taunts, taking the glass.

"Quiet now. Listen. We both know these folks can't hold us. Samantha probably knows as well, so shut up and listen. We hear anything we don't like, I hit them all blind. You psyche them all out and we rabbit."

"We could take them all. They're just . . ." She stops herself.

"Question marks," I say softly. "Human or otherwise. We don't know what we're dealing with. And the last thing that Narayana is . . . is human. Gain info, that's the plan. We're not here for slap-boxing. We're here for Prentis, yeah?"

"Yeah," she agrees. "Do you think it's him? Making his move?"

"Smells like him. But it's too early to tell."

Nordeen's obsession with Liminals is pathological. His predilection is to attack with another's powers, making his angle of assault and egress always a mystery. He wanted Prentis and Tamara when I broke away three years ago but stayed his hand out of what I assumed was affection for me. Still, he is the boogeyman I trot out to the girls when they complain about training.

Each minute that passes could be another that Prentis's power and mind are being molested by that sadistic lunatic, my mullah in this world. He could be making her do horrible things or turning her into something vile. He could be turning her into me.

"Look sharp," Tam says, co-signing on the two heartbeats and two human-shaped things I feel coming down the hall.

Samantha enters first, followed by a younger, light-skinned Latino guy. He strides with two six-shooters on his hips and a long sword on his back. He's skinny, a bandanna fixes his short black hair, and his arms are lean and well defined. Still, his body only looks human.

Behind him, Narayana wearing a white button-up shirt, and finally Mico, dreads tied up tight, a long flowing tan jacket and a black, almost blouse-like top and some coffee-colored sweat pants. They all sit around the table except Narayana. With a silent cue from Mico, he speaks.

"My patron sent me to find the source of the disturbance. It was my own exuberance that made me attack. For that, I take responsibility. Fault to me, consequences to me." He's comfortable to stop there, but Samantha clears her throat, and he continues. "I apologize."

Mico nods, and Narayana leaves the room with a slight bow.

"He roll over as well?" Tam asks.

"Narayana's been alive for over seven hundred years. That's the first apology he's ever given," the Latino informs us, not judging.

"Who are you?" I laser in on Mico.

"My name is Mico L'Ouverture. I am the vassal of the God of connections."

"Sounds pretentious when you say it like that," the Latino laughs and talks at the same time.

"I can't get all those words together," Tam agrees, and I feel her pulse quicken looking at Mr. Six-shooter. But I don't take my eyes off of Mico.

"Humanity likes to think of itself as the pinnacle of intelligence and consciousness on the planet. Yet it's not even the oldest species. There is a consciousness, an awareness, that's been active on Earth since the dinosaurs were young." Mico speaks like a revivalist preacher as he lights one of the joints Samantha is always puffing on. But unlike her, with one hit his entire being changes. My liminal sight shows him flooded with a thousand other . . . influences. Tamara notices it as well.

"Bloody fucking hell. What's in you?" She coughs, almost leaving her chair.

"All those who've ever consumed the flesh of the god. All their knowledge, all their skill," Mico says with a voice fueled by countless others.

"You smoke your god?" I ask, genuinely curious.

"The god is the connection. The smoke is only a way to its flesh," Samantha tells us gently, watching my face for clues to my reaction. I give her none.

"So everyone who smokes 'connects' with everyone else who smokes?" I'm thinking of the privacies and intimacies I shared with Samantha going through this psychic smoke Internet.

"No. For now, only Mico bears that burden." Referring to himself in the third person does nothing to ease Tamara's concern. "But each is awarded according to the needs of the Manna."

"Manna?" my girl asks.

"Mico's name for the god is Manna Elohim," Bandanna Boy says.

"Food of the gods?" Tam asks. Even I'm a little shocked at her knowledge.

"What? I'm fucking literate."

"It's got needs, this Manna?" I demand.

"I do," the smoke answers from Mico.

"Do you need anything from Prentis?" I feel Tam tense up.

"Yes." I hear the American accent of Mico come out. "But the Manna doesn't take what isn't offered." Mico takes another drag and speaks fully with the smoke's voice.

"Understand, liminal healer. You and mine are not natural enemies. Whether or not we become allies is entirely up to you."

"Narayana," Tamara says, picking the question from my brain. "That's what you call that walking nightmare, right? What is he if not the definition of enemy?"

"True, he is your opposite number. An Alter," Bandanna Boy says, losing his smile for the first time. "He is born of entropy. Designed to increase his parentage and lineage."

"His kind are also natural enemies of the Manna," Samantha adds.

"Narayana," Mico speaks up, separating his voice from the Manna again, "is aiming toward redemption."

"Right," Tamara interrupts. "All this is well and good, but we've got family that's MIA. Mr. and or Miss Smokey, Alter this or that—and I have no idea what you are, Mr. Six-shooter—if you can't be of use, no harm, no foul, but we should probably bounce soon, feel me?"

"It was important you knew who was in the room so you could hear me when I say this," Mico's smoke chides. "We've pooled our resources—from the four winds, to the collected smokers, to the lovers of Samantha. None of them have seen hide nor hair of your sister."

I sigh hard. Only one man could keep Prentis from this collection of power and weirdness. I hate saying his name out loud.

"Nordeen."

Chapter Three

I need to sleep and eat. Growing my own body quickly is some of the most taxing bodywork I do. Combine that with the abyss that is that Narayana cat, not to mention the possibility of facing the old man, and all I want to do is close my eyes after an insane meal. But as soon as the peanut gallery leaves us, the teen that broke London starts in again.

"Bloody hell. That Mico looks familiar, yeah?"

"Sure you could see past the six-shooter?" I ask.

"Who now?"

"Latino with the six-shooters and the bandanna?" I say. Psychics don't casually forget.

"No idea what you're talking about." We debrief the entire conversation only to find a perfect absence around the smirky Latino.

"Another question mark." I pull gently on my eyelids.

"We leaving?"

"Assume everything we've got is compromised: no home, no bank accounts, burned passports. We need to stay off our beaten trails until we lay eyes on Prentis." Sam damn near kicks down the dining hall doors with a massive tray of my favorite foods. The click of her three-inch candy-red heels betrays her mood.

"Yours is outside," Samantha declares to Tamara, who instantly tries to levitate a clutch of grapes off the tray. Sam grabs them in mid-air. My daughter takes my head nod as permission to gain distance, but not before getting one last dig in. "No easy journeys to other realms, you two."

I fix a plate of chicken, potatoes, steak pie, grapes, baked beans, and almonds, and a glass of red wine. I manage a quick thanks before I start my seven-minute race to the ends of the plate. My Ethiopian waits until I'm done to speak.

"I'd like you to take a walk with me."

"This your idea or your smoke god's? Or Mico's?"

"You keep acting like I've wronged you, Taggert. What was my offense?" She's trying to muffle her pheromones of rage and ire as she stands over me.

"You keep a secret this big from me and expect what? Thanks? I thought we were in this together."

"You're an idiot." She turns to leave me. I think about stopping her, seizing up her calf muscles so she can't move. But we'd never recover from that. So instead I follow.

Sam is halfway around the outside of the hotel, moving at a furious pace, by the time the early evening London air hits my lungs. Strangers gain tension watching me chase her, like they know our particulars. It aggravates me so much that I'm in a near fury when I catch up with my kind of part-time lover. "How the fuck am I an idiot?" I grab her arm.

"You're so used to the world being against you, you can't see a host of allies laid before your feet," she snaps back, pulling her arm away. "That's what makes you a fucking idiot."

"Sorry for not recognizing a half-naked . . . what did you call him, Alter? . . . as an ally as he attacked my daughter."

"You mean your half-crazy psychotic psychic of a daughter who hates me for no good reason? She's lucky it was Narayana who found her as opposed to darker powers. I told you what would happen if you didn't train her, Taggert," she shouts.

"I was. I am. Both of them."

19

"Training them to hide. To fight. To steal. To disappear in plain sight. To kill. I'm sure they're both savage warriors. But neither of them knows how to live, you pathetic bastard. Now you've got one too powerful to sneeze without causing a telepathic citywide melt-down. The other—gods only know where she is. But I'm the one who has messed up?"

"What do you want? What the fuck do you all want?" I'm not talking to her.

It's the encircling group of Eel Pie residents. Young and old. Indian, African, Saxon, able-bodied, crutched, wheelchair-bound.

"They're just concerned for me," Sam says. I know her phero-mones' effects on large groups of people. I've seen the near narcotic haze folks get into under her thrall. This isn't that. Their eyes are clear. An older Rasta, bundled against the Thames night air in a dark wool pullover and sweats, nearly offers me a joint. Before I can refuse, he speaks.

"Nah Manna fa you, healer. Thy man nah properly prepared, zene? Just spliff fa ta ease tension, quicken thy thought." He's nearly suffused with the reek of the Manna.

"Respect, Bingy man," Samantha says, swiping the joint from his outstretched hand. She takes an impossibly large hit and speaks with smoke issuing from her mouth. "Though I doubt the healer will know how to take such kindness."

I take the offered joint from her hand and match her intake with all eyes on me. Even with my natural resistance to poisoning, I feel the sedative effect the instant it touches my lungs. The Bingy man smiles appreciatively, and I know this is his personal strain. He walks down the block just in front of us. I can't think of a reason to stop him.

An older white woman with clay caked between her fingers offers us a place to sit by her house, underneath a yellow umbrella table. Half the assembled leave. A young Chinese man pours us tea from another house then walks away. All this happens in an unspoken, near liturgical precision. Like Mico and the car.

"The Manna?" I ask Sam.

"It helps with coordination of action."

"It tells you what to do?"

"More like it suggests, shows possibilities. It takes a certain level of familiarity with Manna in order to be aware of its guidance and desires."

I have to ask. "Why didn't you tell me about this before?"

"I was given permission to bring you in one time. Just before your last confrontation with Nordeen, do you remember? You refused. You said you didn't have time for my god, as though I were introducing you to my favorite band. After that, the Manna was silent regarding you." And after a moment of silence. "And why didn't you introduce me to Tamara and Prentis? We have separate lives."

"Tamara has . . . mommy issues." And then. "You didn't tell me what your 'god' was."

"When a four-billion-year-old sentient tuber fungus tells you to keep a secret, you listen," she tells me after taking another hit. I nod, barely understanding. "I told you before that it was my god, the Manna, that secured my freedom from Nordeen. It made its presence known to me even before Mico. For years it wanted to meet you. Prentis and Tamara as well. But it has rules, boundaries it puts in place for what it calls 'healthy growth.' You grow toward the Manna, it doesn't grow to you. You weren't ready. Still aren't, for all that it is . . . ."

"YES I!" Bingy man throws in from a nearby seat.

"But I pleaded with Mico to find Tamara when I felt her distress."

"And I gave you shit for the help." I sigh. "I don't know how to apologize for this one."

"Stay and speak with Mico," Samantha asks, placing her hand on mine. I feel her flood of relief infect me. "He is a friend in need of someone like you; neither follower nor foe."

"I've got to find Prentis."

"You know where she is? Are you prepared to square off against the Razor Necks and him with your only child as your only backup?"

21

Again with the logic. "Stay. Rest. Speak. This is the price of your unwarranted castigations."

She stands, 5'3" max, gives Bingy man a pound, places her hand on her chest and talks toward the docks. Not thirty steps away, three young women surround her, rubbing Samantha's back, holding her hand. I'm left with the Rasta.

"Righteous spliff." I'm supremely tired.

"Respect, healer. I and I's discretion is appreciated, zene?" he both asks and states.

"You one of them Rastas straight out of Ulverston?" I say more as an excuse to stare at him with my liminal eyes, looking for his ailment.

"Cha! Portmore born, Blue Mountain raise, ya nah test I man pedigree!" He unleashes his proud locks from his large knit hat. They frame his jawed face like a protective halo.

"No offense meant." I try to smile, but the arrhythmia in his heart, the lower-than-normal oxygen count in his lungs, are distracting. On instinct I reach to heal him. But the Rasta's dirt encrusted hands grab my arm. His eyes mist but don't cry.

"Old growth make way for new shoots, yah?" Years ago I would have fought him over the idea, but I remember the tribe of poor Africans that told me a healer was a poison to the warrior spirit, and how that almost broke me. Now, after all I've seen, I know there's worse than death.

"Will you ask your god for help?"

"Jah Manna need be asking fa no thing. Jah Manna provide all that's needed."

"Fucking Mico is Jah Puba!" Tamara barks, running up to the table from nowhere.

"Meaning what?" I ask, watching Bingy grin. Wide.

"Tag, Jah Puba is the DJ remix master to end all. He's done everyone in every genre. You want a banger in the streets and the clubs, he's the one you come to. He releases everything free. He's the one

Prentis is always talking about wanting to see. Come on! You can't be this culturally deaf, can ya?"

"Ay, gal. Fay a want to see him lab tail yaself to I man," Bingy announces, giving me a pound then walking back to the hotel.

"I don't speak Jamaican . . ." Tam starts.

"He's saying if you want to see Mico's studio, follow him." She's wild, dangerous, and powerful. But she's also eighteen, beautiful, deviously smart, determined, and the only part of her mother I have left. Seeing her excited, on the edge of happy, I can almost block out the sounds of the oncoming storm.

"Can I go?" Like I could stop her.

"The Rasta is okay, but play safe."

"No play. All research." She smiles, then launches herself after the Dread.

I make my way back to the hotel and find a spare room to crash in, with a wide brass bed frame and functional drapes. All the secrets of my past molest my dreams, as usual. I swear, if my body didn't need sleep, I never would. I'd already been going for days on three hours of sleep when Prentis disappeared. Prentis.

If Tamara is my daughter of blood, Prentis is mine by choice. We both grew up unwanted and abandoned. Both of us were taken by the wrong type of family, abused and used for our power. Tamara may have dealt the killing blow to the insane illusionist who menaced Prentis, but it was my set-up. I offered Prentis safety, security, and our version of a healthy family. And I'm the one who promised I'd never let her go.

I wake to the Egyptian musical mother of protest, the Star of the East, Umm Kuhtlun, being supported by a bass-heavy Tamil beat. Even before I leave the room I feel the massive amounts of activity going on in the old ballroom directly across from the room Tam and

I waited in earlier. Crack levels of dopamine highs tell me no one is in trouble, but that doesn't dull the impact of opening the main doors of the ballroom and seeing every member of Mico's Eel Pie collective in full party mode. It's a Wednesday night.

Not like they care. From the poised supermodel to the awkward elderly, the ingénue to the infant, all are dancing, rolling, laughing like they've got something to prove and nothing to lose. I catch sight of Bingy man, who covertly flips a Manna joint to regular hash and hands it to me. I give thanks but am immediately assailed by four young half-dressed women; dancing like it's their last night on Earth.

The music transitions to a dubstep version of a song I've heard Prentis play, by an American: "Our Paths Will Cross Again." It's a perfect hillbilly dirge, and unlike most girls this age, these girls' moves aren't about simulating sex on the dance floor. They are actually listening to the music, vibing out, loving it. I look past the three hundred hearts and hands to see Mico on a distant stage in a similar near-trance; only he has the presence of mind to throw a head nod my way. It's only after a dulcimer-influenced version of Tricky's "Ghetto Youth" gets in full swing that I can stop looking at all the bodies breathing, moving, and coordinating in silent syncopation, as a somatic firework display. Samantha sees my wonder and joins me.

"I've never seen you dance before," she says softly, her lips brushing against my ear. "Does it take four nubiles to motivate you?"

"I've never heard music done like this before." I didn't even realize I was dancing.

"Not live. But you've heard Mico's mixes coming from my speakers. You like?"

I nod and smile.

"Let's hope Tamara feels the same." I go cold. I scan the room. I know that girl's bio-rhythms better than I know my own. She's gone. Hide and seek. I push myself and scan the unique heartbeats of three-quarters of London. Gone. I run to the room I was sleeping in, registering what the music distracted me from earlier. A note posted outside the door. Written in Tamara's chaotic scribble.

I know he scares you. I know you're afraid of taking me into battle with him.

And I know you'd never let Prentis go. So I'm going after him solo. You've trained me well, Tag. Sit back and let me handle this. If I need help, I'll call. But I can't stand around and do nothing while Prentis is in his grip. You've done enough, Taggert.

Play back-up on this one. I'll play it smart, promise.

Love you.

Chapter Four

"Razor Necks play murder tag for fun!" I shout at Sam as she stands in front of a small dock. There's a boat on the other side of her that I'm meant to be on.

"I know. They used me as a toy for a while. I can't go with you . . . ," she says, trying to calm my fury.

"You know I've got to go."

"And do what?" she demands with her eyes. "That whole crew plus Nordeen, you're going to take them on by yourself?"

"Give me another option!"

"Fulfill your promise. Speak with Mico."

"He's not a fighter. He's too busy spinning world beats for his rainbow coalition of sensitive mushroom smokers."

"Mico would like to see you." I almost flash on Narayana. Tamara is the only one that's ever able to sneak up on me; only one with an actual heartbeat or a need to breathe, that is. But this Alter—still confused as to what that means, exactly—keeps getting the drop on me.

"And if I don't want to see him?"

"I will go back and tell him so. Perhaps it will take that long for Nordeen's forces to arrange your bones." The killer shadow begins to walk back to the hotel.

"Wait!" I shout as I follow him with Sam by my side.

Another DJ is on the decks as I re-enter. The music is good enough but not the same. Not as . . . honest. It's the difference between how Prentis lives and breathes for her music and how I hear a good tune every now and then and forget it. Prentis.

Behind the stage a small circular staircase takes us to a basement. My ears perk as we enter an oval hallway the length of the hotel. In the room at the end I can hear arguing. It's the forgettable Latino and Mico.

". . . he loses; you lose him, you lose Tamara, you lose Prentis." The Latino is shouting.

"I don't have them now!" Mico snaps back. "And if he wins then he's allied with us. His debts become ours."

"No. I've been doing this longer than you. The smoke was smart. You offered him sanctuary. Now—he wins, same sanctuary. It's still their aggression if they move for him on your sacred ground, here."

"And then what?" The DJ sounds exhausted. "We're not ready for Nordeen, let alone his masters."

"Nordeen doesn't have masters," I say, entering the exposed-brick room.

"You know better than that," the Latino says in a way-too-familiar tone.

"Who the hell are you?"

"Seven years ago, a dock in South Africa. You waited until dawn for Nordeen. Two went into that storage container. One came out. The one that went in was an Alter like Narayana, only weak, early in its 'life.'"

"You weren't there."

"You didn't see me." He offers his hand. "My name is A.C. I'm a child of the wind. I'm the reason you can't find your keys one minute, then see them right in front of you the next. I'm the human-shaped flash in your peripheral vision that disappears as soon as you focus on it. I'm nowhere and just on the fringe of everywhere. Always."

Like I need another question mark. My eyes find Mico's. I walk past A.C. and offer my hand to the DJ.

"Me and mine have been a bit gruff with your hospitality. For all you've done, thanks. I won't ask for any more. I've got to find my girl right now."

"If I could help, I would. I have no interest in seeing you back in Nordeen's sway," he tells me, grabbing my hand with both of his.

"Is that all you're afraid of?" I almost laugh as I survey the room. "Nordeen wouldn't take me back if I begged. He's going to yank my throat out if I don't pull this off."

"And that would be the grander tragedy," Mico says, still gripping my hand hard. "If I ally with you, Nordeen's people get to take offense. That means Alters worse than Narayana would be free and clear to come here and slaughter everyone. There are more potential victims than warriors that call the Manna god right now. I can't let this island turn into our Masada." Everything in his earthly body convinces me he's telling the truth. I'm about to let him off the hook, tell him it's okay. . . .

"I can fight by your side." A.C. was right: I almost forgot him. Mico obviously didn't. He crosses me to speak with A.C.

"But you've smoked the Manna," the DJ says softly.

"You think that's the first god I've inhaled?" The wind boy isn't taking things seriously, if his smirk is any indication.

"They'll know you've allied yourself with me," Mico snaps.

"They will not," Narayana says from behind his boss. "Alters are born of stillness, the quiet of entropy. The wind child is born of noise and perpetual movement. Just as I am an affront to the Liminal eye, no Alter will spend time sourcing the origins of his annoyance." Aside from the apology, it's the most I've heard the Indian speak. His voice sounds like dead leaves being pushed along broken concrete with an old rake.

"See? All good," A.C. says to Mico. Then to me: "I'm yours if you'll have me."

28

"Know how to fight?"

"I've been trained by the sickest djinn ever to walk the terrestrial planes. Plus I rock entropy weapons." Again that annoying smile.

"I'll take that as a yes. Let's go."

"You planning on taking a flight?" the smirker says, checking his six-shooters and the three-foot-long sword he secreted behind his back, under his trench coat.

"You gonna blow us there?"

"After a fashion. I can get us dead smack into the middle of your little Razor Neck terror town sight unseen. It'll be a rough ride, but we'll lose no time."

"Do it."

"You might want to get your game face on," he recommends.

I grow five layers of skin quickly, then cut off all circulation to them. Razor Necks are all blade specialists. Those that didn't train me, I trained. First line of defense will always be blades with them. I get sliced now, it's just dead skin. Autonomically my body steps up my bone density to compensate for the weight. Rather than bulk up my muscles I super-myelinate them and dull the rest of my muscular autonomic functions. Once we're there I'll let normal synaptic functions flow, giving me a reaction time five times faster than your average cheetah. I bump my oxygen flow for good measure and grow thin, removable reticulating lenses over my eyelids. A lot can happen in the darkness of a blink. It was Prentis who convinced me to try this trick for the first time. Prentis. And Tamara.

"Ready," I say, standing in front of the assembled crew. "What? Do I have to click my heels three times?"

"I guess this would be a homecoming for you," the wind boy says, stretching out his neck and arms. I catch a nervous, silent "good luck" dance across Samantha's mouth.

"Stay focused on your daughter: her smell, the sound of her voice, the silhouette of her body. Allow yourself to be carried to closer versions of her. You've got to let yourself be taken by the wind."

There's a gust in my eyes, and my reticulating lenses go nuts. Still, I miss nothing. In under ten seconds the light gust feels like a Class 3 hurricane. But nothing else in the room—no furniture, no people— is being affected. I'm fighting to stay upright, but no one else seems bothered. The winds whips so hard I can't even breathe. Just when I start thinking I've been tricked somehow, A.C.'s voice approaches from everywhere.

"You've got to let go." He echoes with desperation. I can't even ask "Let go of what?" because the vindictive wind that threatened to knock me over does. The only thing I can release is my balance. So with a memory of Tamara knocking me out of a twelve-story window almost four years ago, I let go of my questionable balance and fall.

Ground does not stop me. Physics takes a strong bong hit as my falling becomes propulsion. With never-blinking eyes I see only the essence of movement. No landmarks aid my sense of place; every- thing echoes off itself, even my own breath. Only the vague awareness of A.C. in control counters my soul panic, and only in part. When the world makes sense again I'm on all fours in the middle of Razor Neck central, our—their—small, semi-abandoned fishing village on the Mediterranean coast of Morocco. Biya. I'm back in Biya.

The familiar sun-bleached and blue-tile three-story buildings around me represented kitchen, living room, and office to me for over a decade. The smell of fresh fish in the sea-laden air would make me nostalgic, if I had the time. I'm missing two kids.

"Now would be a good time to stand up, Healer." I look up to see A.C.'s sword drawn.

"Don't," I tell him once I see who's coming. Hasan. In the old days he was a friend, in and out of combat. I don't expect loyalty from him now, but I don't want him dead. I give him crippling leg cramps, feel the lactic acid build in his heels and seize his calves fully. The barrel-chested Berber stumbles . . . but stands again and keeps coming.

"You okay?" A.C. asks.

"The problem is not on this end," I say, flooding Hasan's brain with orgasm levels of opioids. Still he doesn't stop. I scan his body, and aside from a monumental infection of hookworms he seems human as ever. "What the fuck?"

"I got this." In the time it takes me to say "No," A.C. has already covered the seven meters to Hasan in the middle of the Biya courtyard. I'm moving toward the both of them as Hasan attacks, scooping upwards with a curved blade in his right hand. Without a staggered step to the right, A.C. would have been gutted from crotch to gullet. Hasan compensates perfectly, placing his left hand at the butt of his knife and going for A.C.'s thorax. The wind boy parries with the handle of his sword casually, then rotates the entire weapon into Hasan using nothing more than the Berber's own force and his finger. But when I scan for wounds, I find none. A.C. sees my confusion as we stand over the passed-out Hasan.

"Entropy blade." A.C. smirks. "Really good at cutting things that shouldn't exist, like a bond between an Alter and a human."

"There's an Alter here?"

"One of the worst. One of the pestilence twins. The Rat Queen. Poppy by name. She makes minions out of millions. It's damn near impossible for an average person not to be infected by her or her brother."

"Twins? How do you know both of them aren't here?"

"'Cause Africa wouldn't be standing. Nah, I've seen Poppy's work before. This is her," A.C. tells me while squatting over Hasan, checking his vitals.

"But your sword kicks them out?"

"Nope. Just breaks the connection. It was your healer-in-reverse move that knocked him out."

"Then we might have some problems," I tell him, pointing across the courtyard at the thirty-five Razor Necks with guns and blades drawn. They start running with psychotic intent.

"Delaying tactic," I grumble, densing up the bones in my hands.

31

"I got this," A.C. says, switching his sword in his hand casually. "Get your girl so we can get gone. Go do what you do best, healer."

I thank him in the only way I have time to. Half the Razor Neck crew goes hysterically blind. The other half collectively develop a maddening tinnitus. It won't stop them, but it'll make them easier targets.

I strengthen my legs and take an old-school Incredible Hulk leap onto Nordeen's roof, three stories straight up. The furniture, the carpet, the smell of mint tea, the ceramic fire stand; it's all here. But no Nordeen. Even his countless jackets. I want to scream in rage but I hear A.C. fighting for his life below me and there's no time. I run to the opposite ledge and use my liminal eyes to scan for Tamara. Two buildings over from where I'm standing. Hasan's old spot. The second floor. And she's in pain.

I back up and do a hurried trigonometry body math. In this town, windows never caught on. Only porthole-sized openings that can be closed by wooden blinds. Last time I tried something like this I had a bigger target and was drunk on self-pity. Now it's for my girl. I launch myself off the roof and aim for the porthole with beefed-up fist and neck muscles to cushion the fall. When I see my aim is true I tuck my head and roll into that nine-inch opening like an Olympic diver.

I roll up just as quick. In the living room a pale, frail–looking, eggshell-white woman dressed in black slim pajamas casts a black glow over Tamara by issuing utterances that sound like the rape of words from her mouth. Tamara writhes with each syllable. I launch both my butterfly knives at the widest part of the Pajama Woman's narrow slit eyes. They land and sink deep into her skull. Then she speaks to me.

"I must confess you are a disappointment, Taggert." She pulls the blades out as though she were removing sand from her eyes. "When Nordeen first found you I told him to put you down. But he begged, and for a while you were good at hunting down your own kind. How he got you to maim and kill them I'll never know. But this breaking my calm and trying to kill me: it simply won't do."

"Leave her alone," I tell the Alter, Poppy, in front of me. What Narayana squelched in himself—that cavity of issuing malaise—this thing celebrates. Her words alone make me sick, mad . . . and engrossed.

"Or what, Taggert? You'll destroy me? I am the nightmare your gods fear." I feel the shock and piercing agony of my two blades going into Tamara. She squirms in inarticulate agony.

"Leave, Taggert. Maybe your daughter's sacrifice will quench my thirst for liminal blood. That's your only hope." She turns from me, bored, and pets Tamara's head, whispering psychotic thoughts in ancient tongues.

I conjure up the Dame's cancer genome and throw it all into the Rat Queen, wishing I had A.C.'s sword. The Alter laughs, and my soul shakes. It stands a full five inches shorter than me and I'm terrified.

"Death abhors my kind as much as life fear us. And here you are with gross material and our antecedents? At your best you are a distraction, Liminal." I see her teeth, a million small rodent-shaped collection. Only they have no calcium deposits connected with them, no nerve endings. These are psychic rat teeth. I'm so fucking out of my depth.

"Where's Prentis? Why did you take her?" I'm stalling for time.

"Why, she's with her uncle Nordeen." It smiles again, and I go cold inside. There's nothing I can do. I have no weapon that hurts, my powers can't . . .

The thought/memory comes borne on A.C.'s errant wind. What he said, what all of Sam's crew has been calling me. How Sam thinks of me. What I am: Healer.

I launch myself at the Alter, grabbing its face and ribs at the same time. Its laugh is terrifying until it senses me trying to correct the essential wrongness of it. Its violation of the human form by existing in it. I pour every drop of my healing into the exploding darkness in it. I put human demands on the human shape, declaring the need for oxygen, circulation, homeostasis, and biology. I push everything into healing the entropy. It wrecks me. It's a losing battle. The darkness infects me, finds a chink in my sense of self and devours me from the marrow outward. It's killing me with my own body. But I don't quit. Poppy roars and throws me off of it.

"You dare . . . ? You liminal filth! I am a daughter of the eternal quiet, sister to the Pestilence King. You dare attempt to heal my nature?"

On the ground, I grin. "It's like you said. At best I'm just a distraction." I felt Tamara awake the second I went deep into the healing. I kept pushing to keep the Poppy bitch's attention on me, so my girl could recover. Didn't take long.

"Bye, bitch." The first time I met Tamara she "shoved" me through a plate-glass window. It was a novice move, but it's still her favorite. Only it's gotten stronger. Tamara combines her telekinesis and her arm strength to shove the Alter hard . . . out, or rather through the house, and the building next to us. And the one after that, through another 600 meters of air before momentum dissipates and drops the Rat Queen deep into the Mediterranean blue. A smart brute-force attack. But even with my quickly closing eyes I can see it took a lot out of Tamara.

"Tag!" She calls my name, almost makes me forget this searing pain.

"Hey, girl. You good?" I touch the loose hair in her face. I want to use my skills to check her, but it burns. You don't touch the void without it touching you.

"Tag, what's wrong?" I hear her say. "Stay awake. Come on, Taggert. I need you. Don't die. Taggert, I can't do this alone!"

I'm so sorry.

Chapter Five

I wake up slowly to a disembodied heartbeat making consistent offerings to an impossible god. Waking slow equals pain; a recently accomplished need for deep healing. I sit quiet for a minute, pinging the bodies around me. I feel Tamara before I see her, sleeping in a chair next to the lush bed I'm in. I'm on Eel Pie. The heartbeat I felt is Mico's people. His is the body that contains . . . multitudes, and it's downstairs in the ballroom with strange children. On the east side of the island, Samantha is sweating profusely but breathing steadily. One more desperately hopeful sweep before I open my eyes. No Prentis.

Muscle decompensation and melatonin deprivation tell me I've been lying down and out of the sun for over three days. I put the rest together pretty easily. No doubt A.C. found Tam and me and did his windy thing before the rat witch could crawl back from the sea. If she could take two blades in the skull, I doubt that would do any more than annoy her.

Those psychic rat teeth plague my memory as I get out of my room quietly so as to not wake Tam. The Alter's words scratch the back of my ears like little rodent feet while I walk down the half-carpeted steps toward Mico. She laughed at my assassination attempt; damn near mocked every move I made. Even Nordeen was never that dismissive of me or my power. She knew Nordeen. Another secret he kept from me.

I open the door to the ballroom to see Mico picking a long-necked banjo, singing to a group of twenty-five children. His dreads are braided back, and he wears black-striped running pants. He's moving a tune too young to be ancient but too seasoned to be an original composition. It's a pliant declaration of unity with friends and family despite whatever may come. Mico doesn't perform, he invites. The same energy he generated with his DJ set he creates with these Eel Pie kids. By the end of the song, even the smallest of them are joining in with handclaps.

"I'm feeling some questions out there," he announces. I'm in the back of the hall, making my way forward along the sides in the shadows among the ever-present scaffoldings. For a second I think he's talking to me.

"He doesn't mean Manna when he says 'smoke them,' does he?" a ten-year-old ginger boy sitting with a coal-black girl five years his junior asks.

"Right. He means cigarettes. It's an old term people used to say when a plane was going down."

"Who doesn't make their living by labor?" an Indian girl of eleven asks, surrounded by little boys and girls waiting to get their hair braided by her. English is obviously her second language.

"Oh." Mico smiles, recalling the lyric. "Making your living by labor means physical work. Sweat equity, we call it around here."

"I know," the little Indian snaps back. "What I mean is, if you do not engage in labor-type work, what other work is there?"

"Rich-people work," another little girl with a Geordie accent interrupts. "The rich, yeah, sit in front of computers and talk phones all day. They'se work in offices. And they don't swear."

"Then how do they eat?" The Indian girl is so confused she stops braiding hair. Her body shows her confusion better than her words. Malnutrition is written all over her digestive system, her calcium-depleted bones, and even her brain.

"They are paid more to sit in offices and make phone calls than farmers or shop keeps or bus drivers," the Newcastle girl continues.

"They must do something very important," the Indian concedes reluctantly.

"Some do. Most don't."

Mico lowers his voice, and all the kids pay attention. "And that's why the Manna has come now. It wants to give us all a choice. An opportunity to change our values. Mr. Whitmore's song 'Hell or High Water' could have been written by any of the smokers here. That's what it means to join with us using the Manna. You love your people, are owned by your people, and the people are owned by you. You love your people and the people love you. It can be a hard road to walk. But the alternative is the solitude people experience now, where the best you can hope for is a soft job in a cushy office doing nothing, watching a screen filling the emptiness of your life with money."

"So Manna hates money?" the Geordie girl asks.

"Manna doesn't hate anything," the ginger protests.

"Right." Mico silences them all. "But money, acquiring the individual wealth and profit, doesn't increase the benefit of all humanity. That's why we work on mutual debt here. I owe you . . ."

"And we can owe you," they say in unison. All of them.

"Okay, my ignoble savages. How many of you have noticed our visitor?" They all turn to look at me with varying degrees of interest.

They all popcorn in a rowdy din.

"What can you all tell me about him?"

"He was sick."

"He's angry."

"It hurts to look at his eyes."

"He hasn't smoked."

"He knows Samantha."

"Ah, but see, I didn't ask each of you. I asked all of you." They close their eyes in harmony, youngest to oldest, and begin humming. After a minute the hum goes hymnal and begins to form consonants and syllables. Two. It takes them longer to figure it out than it takes me.

"Healer," each says in their native tongue and accent at the same time.

"I am so impressed with you all." He's forever genuine when he speaks. He stands and gives the Indian girl his banjo. "Seriously. I don't even think you all will need to smoke when you come of age."

They grumble their displeasure, and Mico laughs. "Go off and teach each other useful things."

"That's the most well-behaved group of mini killers I've ever seen," I tell him slow, unaccustomed to the fatigue in my voice.

"Not all of them are," he says, shaking my hand. "Some are children of the collective. But tell me, how could you tell they had taken lives—the ones that have?"

"Can't mute cortisol depletion or overly taxed trigger fingers. I've been reading fight-or-flight responses since way before Nordeen. I know fighters when I see them. And fighters that young, with that much reflexive behavior? Only way they survived is by killing. You gonna have them kill for your god now?"

He looks at me with pity, and I almost feel ashamed.

"The Manna calls those who need it just as it called Samantha years ago. I am not training baby assassins, even if the Manna were to ask. The children are under our protection. We've pulled them from war-torn lands all over. Sri Lanka, Medellin, Cambodia . . . ."

"Liverpool?"

"Not all wars are public. None of the kids are allowed to smoke until they comprehend the gifts and the burdens. Now. How are you?"

"Standing."

"Despite touching the absent soul of an Alter. You are impressive, healer."

"Your boy was nothing to slouch at." Mico nods with a grin and calls me to walk with him through another door at the end of the ballroom. We descend a narrow flight of stairs to a pantry without windows. Laid out on the table are non-perishable foodstuffs in red wooden bowls.

"Samantha says that you've got to eat a lot after a major healing."
I've half a pound of sunflower seeds down my gullet and ten dried apricots in my hands before I can speak. He doesn't seem shocked.

"The kindness," I call out. "It coming from you, or your god?"

"It's not always easy to distinguish." He considers it while I suck down three boiled duck eggs in under a minute. "In its four billion years of awareness, Manna has never reached out so deliberately to another life form. It's made me . . . crafted me since before my most ancient ancestors ever met. There isn't a thought I've ever generated the Manna hasn't predicted a thousand years before."

"Better question then," I say, biting down on a dark, dry sausage. "Why the kindness in the first place?"

"Initially, Samantha. She refused to share much more than your names before Tamara's . . . tantrum. We knew you were liminal and that you were the one who took Alia down."

I could correct him. Tell him it was Tamara who sliced the illusionist in two. Better he doesn't see her clearly. I can see his annoyance whenever she speaks. If she has to go against this mystery messiah, he'll underestimate her.

"But after we met I recognized you from Manna-induced whispers. Nordeen's former protégé."

"Most smart folks gain distance from anything associated with him."

"Most people aren't engaged in a cold war with his masters."

"And as unaligned Liminals you think Tamara and me would be excellent soldiers in your Manna army."

"Look around you, Taggert. Do you see armaments and battalions? Our war happens decades from now. Neither side dares advance on the other before we're at our maximum strength. Narayana's defection and earlier blows have severely shaken the confidence of the Alters. But in truth, you've met all my allies, and the Alters number in the hundreds. Each impossibly strong, fast, and powerful in terms of trickery and trappings."

"So you want me as general."

"No," Mico says quickly. "I offer friendship."

I want to trust his words, his body, my liminal eyes. But I've got nothing to judge him against. No grown man has ever spoken to me with such naked sincerity before. Every Razor Neck had proper cause to fear me, if for no other reason than my relationship with the boss. And even my enemies' shouts of hate were lies. Usually they were just scared. But Mico stands before me not only unafraid but asking for nothing but good will with the hope that I will reciprocate.

"I'll think about it. But as soon as Tamara wakes up . . ."

"You're on the hunt for Prentis and Nordeen. Samantha said I should bring you to her after you've eaten."

We walk half the length of the island. It's early and the sun hasn't decided to grace the isle with its full presence, sending a typical London gray sky in its place. Inside a weathered pony stable I feel Samantha and a woman with low blood pressure/sugar in a wheelchair, working hard. Their skins are being cooled in the same shape as another person's ambient heat would hit them. A.C. is in that stable with them.

"Yes I! I and I's champion donkey dick herb solidify Jah healer power, WhatIsay?" Bingy man slaps me on my back out of the blue.

"It was some good weed man." I give him a pound.

"Nah the manna you smoke," he says. "Da herb I and I offer over your body as you healed. Raised Zion from the clutches of Babylon, Donkey dick. Yes I!"

"Thanks." I'm so confused.

"Visitations and sightings come upon I and I, with Manna's aid."

"Not the Donkey dick weed?"

"Cha!" he clucks with his tongue. "I man nah receive unknown numbers. Prophecy from sensimilla can nah compare with groundation of the Manna."

"My bad."

"More than bad. To make right, visit I man with the council this evening." He rooster-struts away, gray thick locks swinging from his small head.

"What the fuck was that?" I ask Mico.

"Strange as it sounds, it was an invitation to his house." I block it out and head into the barn.

A.C. must stand for air conditioning. This barn should be hotter. An insulated two-foot bowl rests on a black hearth that juts four feet up from the ground, perfect eye level for someone in a wheelchair. Mrs. Low Blood Sugar/Pressure is that wheelchair-bound person, and her cortisol levels are as high as her temperature should be. The bowl seems to be holding nothing but heat. The wheelchair lady keeps working levers with gloved hands next to the forge, maintaining the heat as jets of steam issue from below the hearth.

"This is the definition of a bad idea," A.C. barks at Samantha.

"Too bad there's nothing you can do to stop it." She pulls my two butterfly knives from a brown sack with a gloved hand, oblivious to our presence.

"I can't keep this heat going forever, you know," the blacksmith says.

"No need," Samantha says as she drops my blades into the forge.

Instantly they melt into a dark and silver mélange. I catch a gasp from Mico, but I'm deep into my own sense of mourning.

They were gifts from Samantha. I spent a few months trying to forget my old life when I took the role of daddy. That meant forgetting my own family, but mostly Nordeen and the savage things he made me do. Samantha bought me the blades so that I might stay in practice. My ability to hurt others wasn't my problem, she told me. It was the inability to choose who I hurt. I got the message, understood where she was coming from at least. But I have no idea what she's doing now.

The blacksmith dons eye protection and stops fiddling with the levers on her right and begins working on ones on the left. The room chills as a silver and black effulgence drains from the forge to a metal cast I can't see.

"I can still see the blood," the blacksmith shouts as she points it out to Samantha.

"That's the point." Sam nods, slipping off her glove and getting closer to the hot, pooled metal.

"Your god cannot be okay with this," A.C. shouts.

"So only elemental children can carry entropy weapons?" she shouts back.

"I shouldn't even have these." A.C. touches his guns. "I'm barely up to the task. Now you want to put them into his hands?"

Sam catches my eye finally and smiles. "He's handled far worse."

Her hit of Manna is deep. With her mouth parallel to the cooling forms, the Ethiopian exhales her smoke. Poppy's blood reacts with the Manna smoke, heating the metal again, only no smoke rises. Quickly the molds go from red to white then threaten to burn though the cooling form. But the smith dunks the whole pan into a vat of ice-cold water. Steam dominates the room until A.C. blows it out. Without form or mold, the blacksmith pulls my two butterfly knives out of the water. But they are different now. Small and curved with a small ring at the end, they look more like an Indonesian kerambit.

"The next time you stab an Alter with these, I promise they will feel it," Samantha says, offering me the blades still wet and hot.

"Not sure I'm worthy of such a gift."

"Then become so."

"Anyone, anything those blades cut will never stop bleeding." A.C. knows how to crush a mood. "Like, forever."

I open them, play with them. They are heavier, yet hold the same balance as before. They fit into my sleeves easier than their previous form, but . . . they don't like being put away. I can feel that in them.

"Taggert will be leaving us soon," Mico announces.

"That's the healer?" The blacksmith perks up. She rolls to me and extends a naked hand. "I'm proud to have forged these for you."

"I'm in your debt." Bingy man's earlier resistance hits me and so I ask, "I'm happy to reciprocate if you'd like."

"I need no healing," the wheelchair-bound smith says with a smile. "But thank you."

Outside of the barn with A.C., Sam, and Mico, I choose to put my mind back on task.

"Your god won't help me. A.C. can't see any further with his wind than Tamara can see with her mind. Mico, unless you've got some skills I don't know about, you guys can't help me any more than you have. And you've done a lot. Tam and I are going to bring some heat down, and your cold war can't tolerate that. So we're gonna cut out. Not as enemies but not as allies. Just . . . acquaintances in a mutual admiration society."

"Alters will be on you like white on rice once you leave this island," A.C. says.

"And we haven't asked the Manna straight out if it would help." Mico adds.

"It's a question worth asking," Samantha chimes in.

"Guess no one heard me say I'm leaving."

"Where?" A.C. asks. "Your Prentis isn't anywhere on Earth. How would you find her?"

"She might be in those subtle realms Samantha has access to," I say quickly. "I'm sure we can find another way to them." Sam can travel to the subtle realms by herself with ease. To carry another, the cost is coitus with Samantha. That's not a toll I'll have Tamara pay.

"Bingy!" Mico blurts out. "He said he has a message for Taggert from the Manna."

Before I protest, Samantha walks into my chest and speaks gently in my ear. "It witnessed the birth and death of thousands of species humans never had names for. It predicted the fall of Atlantis. It grows everywhere on the planet, from tundra to desert. It's as old and mysterious as it is powerful. To have the Manna as your ally is worth the inquiry, my love. I promise."

"He asked for the council," I concede.

"Narayana's off island until tonight," Mico says then asks, "Can you sit on your girl until then?" Speaking as though he were referring to a mad dog. I know her as student, disciple, and daughter. They only see her as the girl who paralyzed London and just tossed an Alter into the sea.

"She'll be fine."

"She's coming." A.C. points at her smiling face as she tries not to run toward me from the Hotel.

"See ya'll tonight." They take the hint and clear out before she gets to me. By the time she's in earshot I slap her across the face hard.

"What the—" She starts. Her cheek is red. Good. She didn't have time to throw up a shield. She felt it.

"What the fuck did you think I would do if you went missing?"

"Taggert?"

"Did you honestly think I would let you walk into any fight, especially with Nordeen, alone?"

"Taggert . . ."

"Don't you know that my life means nothing—less than nothing—without you girls?"

"Taggert . . ."

"What?"

"Why are you crying?"

Bingy man's two-room shack is dwarfed by the wilderness of a backyard he maintains. It feels like its own microclimate; almost completely divorced from its Thames location, it stretches a good half an acre. Clinging vines mix with sloping tropical trees that shouldn't be able to grow anywhere near London to form a canopy that connects the Rasta's low-roofed house to the full garden outside. The dense, perfumed moss is a padded ground covering that invites bare feet. Scents of mint, skunk weed, saffron, and pine dominate different sections of the yard. Denser greenery wraps around the plot providing shelter and warmth. It's the perfect place for the Manna people to throw a party. It's more adult themed than the previous ones, with half-naked men and women lounging in the rare warmth of the evening.

"Fucking all they do is dance," Tam starts as soon as we arrive.

"When your enemy is entropy, it's important to keep spirits up," Samantha corrects.

Ten minutes into the food, drink, and dancing, I see a slight relief in the burden on Tamara's face. Turns out she didn't need my slap. Earlier in the day she let me know dealing with the raw power of an Alter trying to molest, infect, and dissect every atom of her being with rabid, rat-like ferocity was enough to convince her of her mistake.

"They aren't . . . ," she tried to tell me.

"Human?"

"Alive. But more. They only look like people, Tag. They are made of something different, something abhorrent to life. It's not evil. Not bad. That rat bitch is something worse."

I told her that's why we have to be smarter. We're strongest as a team for now, and luckily she agreed. Still, I know I'm going to pay for that slap.

But I'm focused on the slap of Mico's hand on an old seven-string steel guitar as he wails out his version of Jimi Hendrix's "Angel." His singing is like his speech: nothing but sincerity. He's not pure or clean. That's easy to feel. But he fears nothing inside of himself, so he lets everyone see it, feel it, hear it, this naked self. I scan him gently and somehow he feels it and gives a smile of approval. There's a wisdom in the design of his deep structure. His brain operates with an energetic efficiency I've never seen before. He could look brain dead on the wrong scanners, given how little energy his cortex uses, but his glial cells number in the trillions. There's a highway between his audio cortex and the Broca and Wernicke areas of Mico's mind. It's not that he's just a good musician: he hears everything, and feels it all as well.

"Hmmm." Bingy's wearing a gray wifebeater and soccer shorts that go down past his bony chicken knees. He walks up behind Mico from a path no one knew was there, puffing a joint like he was in his homeland and not its colonizer.

"Long time I and I call Mico blood." The garden quiets to a hum at the sound of his pronounced voice. "Babylon would say before Manna. But I man see no place, no where, no when, what Manna na grow. I and I come upon Mico as a young youth, even then him nah touched with Manna and good, as him search for the missing and abandoned him call family. But through the ganja I see him, Mico strong in music true and knowledgeable of the Prophets of the East and West. Yes I! So it's fittin with men of knowledge I expanded my knowledge of plants alongside him. Then what? Decade later still, when the Manna find him, where does Mico return? To one blood. No him and I now, ya zene? Now one blood, now I and I. Jah bless!"

Samantha looks concerned but silently asks us to sit on the moss with her. Many of the low-key group members move to the other scented sections of the field garden to speak and dance. Soon it's mostly the council and us.

"Speak foul thing!" Bingy shouts at Narayana, again slinking in from the shadows.

"You two." The Alter points in our direction with more annoyance than insult. "You impacted that rat queen seriously." I deaden Tam's arm so she can't high five. I heal her quickly when she gets the point.

"The physical violation the girl did only served to heighten the deeper insult of Nordeen's old dog."

"Be civil." Samantha almost rises.

"He speaks the truth," I interject, asking the tame Alter to continue.

"Will she share her insult with the rest of the Alters? Or will that betray too much weakness to them?" Mico asks.

"Only her brother," Narayana responds.

"That's a problem." Tamara jumps when A.C. speaks, again forgetting his presence. "Last time those two got together they almost sunk Sri Lanka. No hyperbole. Literally they almost sunk the whole damn island. The other Alters made a rule that they can't be on the same continent anymore."

"The annoying wind boy is right," Narayana says. "The twins are a threat. But they don't know Manna is involved. Or you, Mico. They are not the biggest concern. Kothar Montague knows what happened. And he is not pleased."

"Who is he?" I ask.

"Alters have different duties," Mico says reluctantly. "Narayana's, for instance, was to sink the wealth of pirates. The rat twins' is to increase the pestilence that feeds on humanity. Kothar's duty, his only reason for existing, is to destroy the Manna."

"He doesn't know if they have any connection to you." Again the Alter points to us. "He's still reeling from the fact that a Liminal could affect an Alter. The last time that happened, it was my daughter."

"'K, quick question here," Tam interrupts. "Your kind, Mr. Scary, you come from like a void of nonexistence right? I get it—more, I feel it. Your whole 'looking like a person, talking and waving your arms around' is like a big 'fuck you' to life. Totally understood. But with all of your kind issuing from the grand Darkness beyond the stars and whatever, how is it you've got children? How's it there's twins and everything?"

"She was my daughter." The Alter's growl of a voice finds its mournful tone. I feel the call of the knives, secured in my sleeves for easy access. He makes one step toward Tamara, I gut him.

"Kothar is smart enough to connect this disturbance of his calm with me, my friend." Mico steps between them, getting on eye level with the Alter. "Though I agree it will take time."

"Go then!" Bingy shouts at Narayana. "Your purpose been served, zene?" The thing in the small-framed Indian body walks away quietly into the bush, and everyone seems to breathe easier.

"Storm clouds in the distance nah disturb the tribe of Judah. For only the judgment day ride upon the sky morning," the Rasta says. "But I and I can connect directly and find the will of Jah Manna, zene?"

He produces three small tubes of a white, gray pulpy material from behind his ear. I recognize the double punch of excitement and caution that flares up in Samantha as the Dread places one in her hands. Bingy lights two. One for himself, one for Mico.

"No god smoke for you?" Tamara asks A.C.

"Me and the mad god Manna have a special connection. Not this public." I can hear his low-level grin.

"Healer," the God says, speaking from Mico's mouth. "You are not my ally."

"True," I say after a few hits in the arm from Tamara. I was caught up in the full-body transformation my liminal sight privileges me to in Mico's body. Every molecule in his body is infused with the Manna. His body is designed for this 'possession'.

"Yet you ask for favor," it says from Bingy's mouth. While it's throughout Bingy's body as well, the efficiency of the domination is not so complete as it is with Mico. "While at the same time foment-ing disobedience in my children." I look over and see Samantha with the unlit manna joint in her hands.

"I didn't tell her . . . ."

"Of course not, healer," Mico-Manna says. "You take no active stance unless it involves your children. Why should I behave any dif-ferently? You ask for my resources but offer none of your own. You are selfish."

"Hold on!" The shrill posh accent of old lets me know Tamara is pissed. "Taggert's a bit of a bell end, no sense denying that. But you're out your ancient mushroom godhead if you call him selfish. Look at him! Man can barely dress himself. Selfish means you take for yourself, yeah? So what's he got to show for all his selfishness then? He's here, I'm here for one reason: she's 5'6" nine stone four if she's eaten that day, pale as an albino's ass, and is so confused about fashion she thinks pink ponytails equal riot-girl chic. Her name is Prentis and she's my friend. Say what you will about me, even the old man if you must, but that girl's been through enough. They call you the god of connections—well, help us connect then."

"No!" it says, and fades from their bodies.

"You are quite brave," Sam says rubbing Tamara's back. Not like my girl will tolerate that for long.

"Fat bloody good it did," Tam says, shrugging the Ethiopian off more gently than I thought she would.

"Y'ah a teach ya seed proper!" Bingy accuses me as I stand.

"She's got her own mind, her own voice. It's obvious your god isn't feeling either, so . . . ."

"You track blood to the door of the god then ask for help?" Bingy barks, angry.

"I'm to blame," Samantha says, getting between us. "I made Mico bring them here."

"Me nah protest the aid, but the manners. When Manna speak, noneya listen."

"I heard," Mico interrupts deftly. "The Manna wants something from you, Taggert."

"What? What does it want? Seriously, this shit is getting on my last nerve. Billions of years old and it hasn't learned to ask for what it wants?"

"The time has come for Bingy man, the true rough of Portmore to lay down his burden," Bingy says, sitting on a large boulder covered in a light red moss.

"What are you talking about?" Mico is the first to his side.

"In the west, Babylon doctor call it Parkinson's Disease. But true Rasta nah call his body by no other name than Jah Rastafari."

"Can you heal him?" Sam asks. I nod but gesture to Bingy. He shakes his head no. With a gentle grip, he embraces Mico's cheeks with one hand.

"See, a new tender for the Manna is now required. In I and I vision, him a liminal. Known by that man healer him."

"Both/and." Mico's desperation is slight in his voice but heavy in his body. "We find the new root tender and you are healed. We can do that."

"I sacrifice only my skill, nah my life, blood. And sacrifice is what Manna need in order to aid them that need it." They all see his hand shake for the first time as he points to us.

"I have no idea what's going on," Tamara says, stretching her legs. "You're telling me old dread thinks if we find a new tender, whatever that is, your god will help us?"

"His name is Bingy. It's short for Nyabinghi, a celebration of life and love that happens among certain True Rasta people around the world. The tender is someone who sees to the physical needs of the Manna's growth. It needs to be shaped, manicured, and coaxed in order for us to use it appropriately. That is his calling, his purpose in life. He's refusing aid from Taggert because he believes another person, a liminal your father knows, would do that job better. I'm trying to treat you as a guest in the house of my god, Tamara Bridgecombe. Do me a favor and start acting as such." Mico's fury, contained as it is, has me reaching for the blades again, given that he's a nose hair away from Tamara. But my girl surprises me.

"I'm sorry." She's soft when she says it. I circle over to Bingy and offer my hand. Hesitantly, he accepts it.

"Thank you. But this may be a moot point. I crippled or killed almost all the liminals I met when I was with Nordeen."

I didn't mean for it to sound as harsh as it did. But they all stare at me hard. It's their fault for calling me healer all the time. Nordeen called me something else. My girl isn't fazed.

"What about the African?" Tam shouts.

"Want to be more specific?"

"Before Nordeen. You told me and Prentis about the little kid. . . ."

"Who could make things grow." The barefooted Mogadishu kid crawls from my memory.

"Yes I!" Bingy nods triumphantly.

"Hold on. I don't even know if he's still alive."

"Got a name?" Mico asks, already on a cell phone.

"Ahmadi Suleiman. His dad ran a cell phone company in Somalia. But that was over ten years ago."

"It's enough," Mico says. "Pack your bags. We're going to Somalia."

Chapter Six

In under an hour Mico had us helicoptered off the island. A far classier ride than any of the rock hoppers Nordeen ever had me in. Sam, Bingy, A.C., and some of the more conservatively dressed followers of the Manna jumped on the helicopter for the transport directly to Heathrow. Bingy and Mico argued in hushed tones while Sam calmed the followers. As good as the helicopter was, it's nothing compared to the jet. It's plush, air-conditioned, with room for fifteen easily. Narayana disappeared after a whisper from Mico.

I opt for rest on the plane, not out of fatigue, just preparation. I don't like what happened at Nordeen's. Poppy didn't so much hurt me as shake my skill, my powers. Plus, I'm not sure what these micro tremors I keep feeling mean whenever I yearn for my knives. The healer in me is not a fan of A.C.'s comment: "They never stop bleeding." I shut out the world and retreat into body meditations that go so deep they might as well be called sleep.

I'm searching for stray incipient bacterial infections in the humans' stomach linings as I review my near-death experience. Hasan was a damn-near vegetarian. Before Nordeen got his claws on him, word was he was studying to be an imam. He held on to physical cleanliness with a desperate passion, to compensate for the Nordeen damage. So where the hell did he get hookworms from? Tam's flirting from the seat behind me interrupts my meditation. I keep what concrete thoughts I have on the bodies so she can't pick up on my ear hustling.

". . . you being Mr. Wind Man, yeah?" she says with her street-tough accent. "Figured you to just fly us to Africa."

"Propriety must be observed, Ms. Bridgecombe. This is a Manna mission. That means Mico has to figure his way to the Mog. Now, when you were in jeopardy, well, that was an affront to nature itself. I had to intervene." I feel A.C. take a drink of something.

"Thought you was part of his crew. Inner council, ennit?"

"To a degree. I've got loyalties but I'm non-monogamous. That's the thing with giving your life to an elemental force. They are jealous and forgetful lovers. The wind will allow me to have other friends, paramours even, so long as it's not a big deal. But once I get serious, that's when the wind comes and sweeps all memory of me away."

"You telling me you're fucking a cyclone?" I'm embarrassed as a parent.

"Not in the physical sense. But when I was younger I was given the option of being trained by the wind to fight and thrive. To know and make others forget. It was an honor, so I said 'Yes.' But I was too young to understand the full weight of my decision."

"So you're not Liminal?" She sucks her teeth hard at him. "Thought you was something special." There's a warmth in his weight as he leans back in his chair.

In the back of the plane Bingy fills his lungs with a mix of his god and marijuana. The humans sleep deeply and quietly through the night flight. Sam's ears are occupied with a low meditated hum coming through headphones. Mico music. It's only in the cockpit that I feel any tension. I pop up quickly and head there.

"You OK?" I ask past the salt-and-peppered Arab of fifty years or so who opens the door.

"I'm fine," Mico says from the co-pilot's seat.

"Wasn't talking to you." I'm looking at the pilot. She's that golden brown you can only get from living under a Saharan sun. Strength stakes its uncontested claim to her small oval face, but there's not a hint of muscular rigidity. Her blue-rimmed black eyes belie a practical genius as they dart from me to the plane's instruments, to the sky, to Mico, then back to me in under a second.

"You're the one with the friend in Mogadishu, right?" Her voice is deliberate, speaking in a non-native tongue.

"Something like that."

"If you're really his friend don't introduce him to this one." She signals toward Mico then turns her attention back to piloting. Mico has nothing but sadness in him now.

"Perhaps it is better we go to sit down, yes?" The elder Arab, I see in his bones, in the same blue-rimmed black eyes, is the pilot's father. As I go back to my seat he makes his rounds to the council. After a minute or two he sits with me.

"You are known healer," the older man says. "Salaam. I am Munji Ibn Shah."

"Might be better you call me Taggert," I tell him, taking his hand and feeling the Manna throughout his body.

"From back in your days with the demon Nordeen, do you remember the Men of the Shah?"

"Hash dealers along the Moroccan Atlantic. Had contracts in Marseilles and Brighton as well, right?" I'm remembering with an approximation of fondness.

"You see? That was me, Fatima, my daughter, and even Mico for a time. We are old business associates."

"You guys ran a tight ship. Nordeen always complained you made enough noise to be annoying but not enough to be worth dealing with."

"I call that the sweet spot." He laughs. "My daughter disagrees. She would prefer to go totally unnoticed."

"She seems angry."

"That's only because Mico is around." He keeps laughing. A.C. joins in from the back seat. "Maybe you can heal some of the hurt from her heart."

"My skills don't work that way." He sounds a bit too sincere in his request. But the old man is already on his knees on the chair looking over at Tamara.

"Well, then maybe it is for this young beauty to help me. Munji Ibn Shah, at your service."

"Wot?" my girl says, half stunned.

"Your power and beauty precede you, my dear. Tamara, she who drowned an Alter, may Allah curse their names for a thousand years, no?"

"'Ear that, Tag? Proper respect."

I feel the yawn of the plane and know we're heading east. It's the smart flight plan. Going anywhere near the Mediterranean might tip off the Alters. But straight south from London, like we're heading to Morocco, then southeast, gives us proper traffic camouflage.

I keep listening for a while as Hasan and A.C. take turns mildly flirting with my girl. She eats it up. Feeling valued and coveted is rarer than it should be. I'd rather she feel their respect and admiration than the weight I've got right now. It's not just Prentis. A.C. was right: these blades should not exist. I feel their desire to spin and cut even when I'm still. They call from that illustrated abyss that I touched in Poppy. My arms keep tensing against their absent weight.

We land in Kufra, the most southeasterly series of oases in Libya. Ibn Shah tells us we're here to refuel, so we've got time to stretch our legs. We're all happy for the fresh air, hot as it is. I've been here once before, barefoot and savaged from a life of service to a proto-human warlord. It's a destination point for Sub-Saharans trying to make their way north, which means it's a recruiting post for pimps and Al Shabab proselytizers. That's what I'm prepped for when I get off the plane in the desert morning sun and see three jeeps approaching from the western hinterlands, loaded with men with weapons drawn. Nomads.

"We good?" Tam asks me. I mean to point with my finger but a blade rests in my hand as I gesture. I understand the completeness of her question when I spy A.C. out of the corner of my eye with his hand on his hilt.

"The nightmares of demons speak your name in hushed tones," Samantha's soothing voice whispers behind me. "The god of connections is cautious of you and your lineage. Is your will to be consumed by mere weapons?" I feel the choice—that thing inside of me that is entirely too stupid to ever stop fighting—flex. I slap the blade closed and pocket it.

"And what's that one doing now?" Tamara asks. From the three-room excuse for an airport, Fatima drives out, alone, to intercept the jeeps in an old Volkswagen Thing.

"I'll go," Tam says and starts levitating.

"Not if you value your peace and sanity," Ibn Shah says gently. "Fatima doesn't endure interruptions well."

She's slight, dressed in the style of the West, with exposed arms and slacks. She carries no weapon. But as soon as she steps from her ride, it's clear she's in control.

"Who is she?" I ask Samantha.

"Mico was hers before the Manna," she says. "She's the smuggler princess of the Maghreb. Munji brought Mico into the life, but it was Fatima who schooled him. Together they converted him from privileged American into a card-carrying underground denizen. Legend is, their love was palpable. It is said they possessed each other. They say the three of them were inseparable until he went to the desert."

"What happened in the desert?" Tam asks, looking deep into the vast expanse herself.

"He found the Manna," I tell her.

"He found himself," Sam corrects me.

Turns out the nomads were the water and fuel hookup. The water is ancient and pure. The fuel is sufficient to make it to the Mog.

＊

As soon as Samantha tries to put a head wrap on Tamara it's clear my girl will be staying with the plane. Hijab and Tamara will never go hand in hand. I'm glad. I hear Somalia is safer. They even put lights in the Bakaara market. But one wrong move, and it's Tamara versus Al Shabab. And I don't know how to feel bad for Al Shabab.

"Where to?" Mico asks me as soon as we disembark and clear the outside of the airport. Bingy and Hasan flank him.

"Central Market. But we need a gun crew to get to town." I point to a crew of skinny, shiny black men in camouflage standing by armored vehicles. Before Mico can take five steps, Hasan is making friends using impeccable Benadir, coastal Somali speak. I lived here for years and could never get their cadence right. In under fifteen minutes we've got an escort to town for free.

Take the Grand Market in Istanbul; darken it. Replace tourists with automatic rifles and add more internet shops and you have the outermost layers of the six-block-wide Central Market. The deeper we go, the more I feel the need for the blades. We form a tail of junior pickpockets from jump. The older and wiser know to stay clear, waiting for a long con. I beeline through the crowded market to the site of an old cell-phone shack. The wrinkled woman behind the counter remembers me from the war days and cringes as a digital bell heralds my entrance into the doorway. Samantha carries the sense for both of us and walks behind me, taking my hand. This is her part of the world. She knows the non-verbal language. Hand-holding means she is mine. I'm a family man now. Not a threat. I ask for Ahmadi, her boss's son, and she says, "Lido."

"We're going to the beach," I tell Samantha.

The beaches of Somalia are their greatest national treasure and every Mog kid knows it. I fear the day Europe descends on these white sand shores again. The afternoon tension of the market is quelled by the lapping waves of the Red Sea as shiny little black boys in T-shirts and shorts yell and scream at the ocean, begging it first to carry them away, then return them to shore. Mico's assembled crew sits under a large umbrella provided by a British-educated Somali entrepreneur. He's returned home to participate in the "tourist boom" predicted by all, by opening a beachside cafe. Of course he's in love with Samantha. I grow a complex but subtle mucosal-and-skin-filtering system so I can strain out her pheromones and focus.

Liminal bodies shine, radiate a power barely contained by flesh. In the Nordeen days I trained myself to recognize it from miles away. It's been a while, but after twenty minutes I feel the old tingle, the liminal tug, by a black, gray, and red coral outcropping.

"Found him." I stand.

"Drink coffee," Bingy admonishes Mico as he stands. "Yah an gwan vex da boy by coming in mass. Healer man and I stand sufficient."

Ninety in the shade even with the sea breeze as we walk across the beach and Bingy is unfazed. He lets his dreads fall and children follow us again. This time not to pilfer but to wonder. The prideful stride of the Jamaican makes me want to overhaul his dopamine pathways so that he can keep that strut forever. But there are so many ways to lose a prideful swagger. Bingy marches into the ocean toward the small coral outgrowth almost unconscious of the waves. I wade in behind him, trying to stay standing.

The coral is slippery and sharp as we climb above the water. Ahmadi has the unconscious skill of a Liminal, growing spongy algae to sit on as he focuses on a small thin plume of sea flora sprouting up from the coral. His obliviousness to our presence is predictable. The seventeen-year-old outweighs his peers by fifteen pounds. Malnutrition has never touched him. Even his shirts and shorts are branded. In these lands, Ahmadi is rich, and the affluent are rarely observant. I have to speak to get him to raise his rust-covered head.

"Ahmadi."

"Taggert?" He asks with a distracted smile, then stands and hugs. "You . . . you were a dream of my childhood for years."

"What changed your mind?"

"Whispers on the wind of a healer walking the slave lands." He notices Bingy, then notices something else about him.

"They call him Bingy man. He has an offer for you."

"A . . . a root. I don't know if there are words for what I see." He tries first in Arabic then in Bendairr. Even then, he stutters. "There's a root in a fungus that reacts through him."

"What him say?" Bingy asks. I translate best I can. The Dread nods and bends low to examine Ahmadi's foliage effort. "Ask if him make this from plant?"

"We just saw him do it," I tell him. Bingy stays quiet until I do what he says.

"No, it was in the coral, growing in the spirals of the shells of the dead animals. I just made it strong enough to break through. I was working on making it more tolerant of direct sunlight."

Again I translate. Happy with what he hears, Bingy pulls a Manna joint from his hair and hands it directly to the kid.

"What is it?" Ahmadi asks me but keeps his eyes on the Manna in his hands.

"Him and his friends call it a god."

"Allah?"

"Allah is a word," Bingy says, indicating that I should translate. "Buddha, Jesus, Yahweh, Jah, all dem vocabulary of man. The truth of this world, beyond them vocabulary and written word of man I and I feel with Manna. Dis a true and living god."

I translate it all. Probably badly. Bingy pulls a lighter from his dreads before he speaks again.

"But this choice. You are Liminal, so you cannot smoke casually, or be coerced into such. To smoke I man's Manna is to join will with the Manna. I man be bound for life. No distance, no other loyalty can interrupt the joining."

I'm shocked as I translate. So this is the dance they've been doing with Tamara and me. I was so concerned Mico's people were trying to get us to smoke. In reality, they probably don't want to deal with us forever.

"Have you?" Ahmadi asks.

"Smoked? No. But I know someone who has."

"Is she . . . happier than others?" the kid asks, still not looking at me. He is obsessed.

"No," I say plainly. But then, "She does have more of a sense of place. Purpose. I love her, if that counts for anything."

"You love her but don't share her god?"

"The world is weird. I can't tell you not to smoke. Bingy's people had knowledge of someone like you in the world. I brought them here. Say the word and I'll take them away."

As the kid thinks, he transforms his algae seat into a bouquet of rose-shaped blooms. Still, his attention is locked on the Manna. I translate everything for Bingy as we wait. The Dread just nods and looks out to the setting sun. It takes a while, but the Somali speaks.

"You say they heard about me. How?"

"That one saw you in a vision." I point to Bingy.

"Tell him I saw him in a dream," Ahmadi says. I translate, and Bingy offers the youth the lighter.

"I nah need ya na longer, healer," Bingy says as soon as Ahmadi takes his first hit. "Manna speak the first tongue. Translation nah necessary."

I head back to shore, noting the decreased temperature of the water already. They'll be on that coral for a while. The beginning of the evening cool competes with the ebbing tide for my attention until I hear Mico's familiar, almost flamenco, plucking. Of course Mico and his crew can't keep a low profile to save their own fucking lives. A decent-sized crowd attends the place where surf and sand meet by the ex-pats' café, surrounding a seven-foot bonfire. All of them singing and playing music with more abandon and better percussion than the Eel Pie crew. Still, the Rainbow collective is more synco-pated, coordinated.

"Do you know Zaar?" Munji is on me before I can ask what the hell. I shake my head. "It is as if a bad spirit is in someone and so they must be healed. In truth, the spirit is not bad, it is only that he wants to fight—"

"Whatever," I interrupt. "Bit of a scene, no?"

"This?" He laughs at me. "Wherever Mico goes, he must play music. I would sooner ask you to stop healing."

The old Arab slaps my back—no questioning about Bingy—and escorts me into what looks like part intervention, part séance, with Mico playing chief-therapist-weird-guitar-player. It's a long-neck four-string instrument with a massive half gourd for its body. The girl writhing in the sand and near the ash is small and thin, dressed in a powder-blue dress. She's the cousin of the café owner, accord-ing to Munji. The beachfire lights show her eyes are possessed by a bright red glow. Her deep contortions in the sand scare most of the onlookers. When she plays with the hot coals of the fire in her hands, others cry. Mico keeps playing the music that dements her. She curses in no language I've ever heard, but Mico just sings coolly back to her in Arabic. When she has enough, the girl—the thing inside of her comes for Mico. He shouts a cloud of his smoke in her face. I know it's not English he's speaking just like I know it's not his god speaking. Still I understand.

"Hold fast, Cushite! I am the champion of your mother, nurturer of your entire pantheon. The child you may empower but do not think to harm me. I would have you as my ally, but you would not survive as the enemy of my god."

He says it in perfect rhythm, almost as though the entire encoun-ter were planned, with no halt in his strumming. Samantha reminds the frightened drummers to continue their beats from the periph-ery of the crowd. Mico's lips move, but I can't hear him anymore as he advances toward the thing in the girl. His words are only for It.

The girl's body posture betrays not admonishment but appeasement, compromise, and finally affection. Mico hands the long-necked guitar to another man just before he, the girl, and the spirit inside her hug.

"You see?" Munji says with a characteristically heavy back pat. "Before the spirit plagued the girl. Now he is her ally. He will protect her; aid her family and her generations. Plus we can call on him for aid. Simple."

"Suppose I told you I don't believe in spirits or gods?" He laughs almost non-stop until we make it back to the plane, Ahmadi in willing tow.

"You know the world you're introducing him to?" Fatima, sitting in her pilot's chair, demands of me.

"World of smuggling and border bandits?"

"Far worse, asshole. What happens to that boy is on you now."

Chapter Seven

I'm almost as tired of waiting as Tamara. Our flight back was as direct as a smuggler can get, and Eel Pie Island feels weirdly homey now. But we've done what the smokeable God wanted, despite Fatima's warnings. I'll confess that her declaration reminded me of a younger Ahmadi's words: "I will die without this land." But he was a child then. And if there's one thing adulthood teaches, it's how to live with things that would kill a younger you. But there's no proper script for dealing with Nordeen. No strategy to program. We need to find Prentis. Now.

Mico asked for time to prepare, and given we'd just flown across Africa and back, I had to give it. Tam and I compare notes in a room on the ground floor she's taken for herself.

"Fatima chick got some heat on her toward the whole crew. Notice how she won't step foot near here. Won't let her da' come either."

"He's a smoker. She's not. Look, as Liminals, we smoke this shit and we're locked in, get it?"

"Locked into what?"

"Wish I knew. I'm not sure if they're all hallucinating or . . ."

"An ancient fungus God has a consciousness and a cult?" Tam disses.

"Says the girl who can read minds?"

"It's not that something isn't going on. Just we've only got their version of the story. The other side . . ."

"Is the Alters."

"Speaking of, you alright?" I'm about to say fine when I realize I've been playing with the curved blades again.

"I'll be fine. Just keep your eyes open and your mind shut."

"How's that?"

"Remember the void of the Alters? Well, imagine the opposite. A million and one voices all at once. What did Mico say he could do? Connect with anyone that ever smoked? You want all of that taking residence in your dome?"

"Alright. Just saying you're more OCD with those things than usual, get me?" She wants to back away from me, so I sheathe the blades and instantly feel the better for it. So does she. "You think we made a mistake? Coming here? Trusting Mico and them?"

"Mico, former smuggler, turned DJ, now head mushroom cult leader who trains baby assassins? What the fuck makes you think I trust him?"

"But you just gave that kid Ahmadi to him?"

Three hours later the council meets with us in the underground room with the long rectangular table. If Bingy is to be believed, Ahmadi is resting at his house. Everyone's cortisol is up.

"Manna knows the need," Samantha starts, taking my hand.

"Yes I!" Bingy chimes in. "And him healer man supplied a strong ally."

"A debt is owed," Mico says cautiously, deliberately.

"Go on then. Ask your herb where Prentis is," Tamara demands. I don't know why Mico is so reticent, but he pushes past it and lights the Manna joint. Once again the smoke inaugurates him.

"The animal totem is here." The smoke speaks through him.

"Where?" Tam stands. "On this island? I've checked everywhere."

"But not every when."

"Old God." A.C. stands beside Tamara. "You're saying Prentis was taken out of time?"

"By the unclean Liminal," it says with no disgust. Then, "No."

"No, what?" Samantha asks for some dumb reason.

"No, your god won't help us." I sigh.

"You pointed my children to a kindred spirit. I have done the same. Nothing else is owed, healer."

"Why do you hate me?" It's a genuine question. I can't understand what I've done to piss it off so much.

"You would rip apart space and time for the benefit of one. I will protect my hundreds and their millions by keeping them in proper relation to birth and death. You think too highly of yourself, healer . . . ."

There's a fight in Mico, between spirit and smoke. Then smoke and flesh. He trembles and the table shakes. I see what was once a concerto in his body turn to a free-jazz thrash-metal jam session. It's like a force-of-will hiccup, as though a singular muscle in a body becomes conscious and demands expression. His full lips flatten, his sharp Adam's apple rises, and with his own voice, Mico shouts.

"No!"

No one is secure. Everyone is standing. None of the council has seen Mico like this or ever heard discordance between the man and his God. Even the Alter has a look that approaches fear.

"That's not good," Tam coughs out. I feel her slam her psychic walls down around her brain. Good girl.

"Can someone else . . ." Mico's voice whistles out. Bingy replies quickly and lights a joint. Instantly the God occupies the Jamaican's voice.

"You've forgotten yourself, vassal."

"They haven't done anything wrong!" Mico protests free and clear of his God. "I know you want them on our side, but from the beginning you've treated them like criminals."

"And you would tear asunder plans millions of years in the making for what?"

"For the life of a Liminal lost in time," Mico pleads. "The Liminals exist to hold the important choices of humanity. Why would they choose us if we don't give them a reason?"

The god says nothing through Bingy for a while. I'm thinking it's contemplating until Tam calls its strategy perfectly.

"Are you seriously giving your boy the silent treatment?" She sighs.

"I don't need to explain myself to my vassal." Smoke-filled eyes blink hard.

"You tell them no," Mico says slowly. "But you allow for my dissent."

"Bad line of thinking." A.C. puts his hand gently on his friend's shoulder. "This isn't a mortal you're arguing with. Your cells declared loyalty to the Manna in the desert when you had nothing . . ."

"And I will serve it." Mico turns back to A.C., equally as compassionate. "But the Manna needs human hands, human minds, and spirits to enact its will. Well, maybe it also needs some human compassion."

"It is my compassion for your species, cultivated over the brief moments of consciousness your race has entertained, that has forged every element of your life, Mico L'Ouverture. From your first breath to now. Mind my will, vassal, or watch that compassion evaporate."

"That is a threat from a god. Your god," A.C. points out.

Mico crosses the room to get eye to eye with Bingy-Manna. "But that's my point. We've all felt your power. Me more than most. My volition could be annihilated, but still I'm here saying I want to help . . . and I can."

"You've been indulged for too long. Been given too many freedoms," the god says. "Ask your indulgence from the void what it thinks."

Everyone turns to Narayana, braced by a far wall and shadow. His lips barely move as he speaks. I avert my eyes from the abomination.

"This is the type of trap I would lay. For most, to travel backwards in time is a perversion, one Nordeen would not dare attempt on his own. An Alter guides him. If you follow, you will be out of your time, distant from your power. Should you run into an Alter, especially one strong enough to command Nordeen, you would not have your people to protect you . . ."

"Nor myself to aid you," the Manna speaks.

"Well, mark this day on your calendar, boys and girls," A.C. announces. "The wind, an Alter, and the Manna all agree on something. I'm sorry, Taggert, Tamara. I really am . . ."

"Samantha," Mico barks back. "What do you say?"

I don't envy her. She's seeing the cost of going against her god being played out before her eyes. Yet she knows; no matter what gets decided in this room, I'm going. She struggles to find the diplomatic answer.

"I have no useful council to give," she says gently. "The choice is your own, Mico."

"See!" Mico snaps. "Samantha smoked long before me, has a longer history with the god, and still she has doubts . . ."

"My doubts span both sides," she confesses, trying not to look at me.

"You can stop me. Make it impossible for me to attempt what you know I'm thinking," Mico almost pleads. "But if you don't stop me, I will try. For your sake. For the sake of the lost Liminal."

"For him?" the God asks, pointing at me with Bingy's long black finger. "For this broken healer with delusions of paternity? The discarded tool of the petulant and unclean Liminal?" It's weird to hear yourself described with such casual disregard from the mouth of a God you don't believe in.

"Not for him. For the girl lost in time with Nordeen. The Alters have at least two Liminals now. So do we, with the addition of Ahmadi. Once again, stalemate. But if we—I—can rescue the girl, at worst we weaken their grip. But at best, we gain one ally." He looks toward me and Tam. "Maybe more."

The body of Bingy walks past Mico to me. Inside Bingy's body, the Manna makes the collected rage of humanity seem like a hissy fit as it stares at me. The fury of a million minds work their frustration out in the Jamaican's frame.

"I know how this ends, Healer. And I blame you." The spirit departs Bingy unceremoniously, yet he's the least shaken of us all. The entire council begins talking at once. But Mico isn't hearing any of it. Instead he walks to me and offers his hand.

"Friends?"

"You sure I'm worth it?" I ask, shaking a strong hand.

"You better be."

"Right then. How's this work?" Tam asks.

"Without me," A.C. confesses. He looks like he's aged viciously in the past few minutes. There's no smile in his voice. "I can't . . .this is just a phenomenally bad idea, Mico. The wind is pulling me away from you already."

"A. C.," Mico almost whimpers. "You've gone in time before."

"I'm insubstantial, barely material. The northern wind is my God, and I learned long ago to follow its instructions. And it's telling me to dissipate entirely from here."

"Your name will always be with me," Mico says. "I will always remember you."

"Then maybe, if you survive, we will find each other again."

I feel my memories of . . . whatever was just here disappear before I lose sight of it. Whatever it was lives in that place where that favorite song, that awesome TV show, that joke you can never remember lives.

Bingy, no longer infected by the God, walks away without a word to any of us. It feels like Sam is looking down at me even when she rests her hand on the place where Narayana stabbed my chest. I make sure there's no filtering in place while I inhale her scent fully.

"This is going to be hard for you to remember, Taggert, but please try."

"Okay."

"Your life has just as much value as Prentis's and Tamara's. At least to me. I need you to stay alive. I need you to come back."

"That's the plan." I try to smile.

"Don't delude yourself. There is no plan." She kisses me hard on the mouth then leaves. I watch Narayana whisper into Mico's ear then bow and leave. Finally it's just Mico, Tam, and me in the room. My girl tags me with a psychic message.

"Trust him now?"

"Like we've got a fucking choice."

"You got a TARDIS or something?" Tamara demands as we make our way into the moonless night in front of the hotel.

"The Manna chose me, or maybe 'bred me' is a better way to put it, to be able to make disperate connections. To link things, places, movements that usually wouldn't join." Mico clutches an acoustic guitar like a security blanket.

"How?" she pushes.

"Music," I respond. "It's why he's such a good musician. DJ, even. He can put any two tracks together, right?"

"Exactly. Music was my medium before I became conscious of the Manna. My God won't help, but it's also not taking any part of the knowledge of all those that have smoked before. I've got the memories of at least four chaos mages in my head."

"Wot, you on some magic now?"

"You want science, liminal girl? If I say 'Chirality,' does that mean anything to you who defy classification?"

"Not a bit." I sit on the ground and prepare for a lecture.

"The god of science then. The Big Bang sent every bit of matter that exists or will exist on a journey outward. Only there are no straight lines in nature. Everything is moving and turning at the same time.

Sometimes things, be they planets, atoms, or states of energy, bang into each other. Something new is formed. Something old is re-formed, destroyed. Those impacts are different than the usual trajectory of matter. There's movement and then there's a stop. That's like a beat, understand? The universe is wobbling, and it has a soundtrack. The earth itself hums at a discernable frequency. I can hear the stretching and squeezing of space. Everything is spinning in the same direction. Every molecule in concert, in union with everything else . . ."

"Not the Alters," I chime in, getting only the vaguest sense of what he's talking about.

"Exactly. They are the uncreated. Reality and creation literally spin around them, avoiding them as much as possible. They don't harmonize with the atomic spin of this reality."

"'K, everything spins, save Alters. So what?" Tam demands.

"So they disrupt in a very predictable way. That predictability rubs against the Big Bang reality in a known and familiar interval. It's a discordant rhythm in space and time. I can listen for the disruption."

"So if you can hear the disruption in time, then you can hear where Prentis is?" I ask.

"Big deal!" Tam shouts. "You can hear where she is. How will we get back there?"

"You," Mico tells her. "We only experience time linearly. It's actually more like an extremely long-playing record, cycling through different iterations with slight variances over and over again. It's possible for a strong enough telekinetic like yourself to adjust molecules from one time frame to another. Change our vibration, you change our location. It's no different than moving something in space. Just think of it like matching the vibrations on a guitar string."

"So you point the way and she gets us there," I say. "What do I do?"

"Keep us alive, for one. One misplaced molecule, one excessive vibration, and our bodies could dissolve under the temporal strain. Plus, it will require an insane amount of will."

"Say again?" Tam says. Getting a sense of what's going to be asked of her.

"And keep us sane. Human beings are social creatures, in time as well as biology. Our psyches, brains, and the like are accustomed to this position in the flow of the universe. I don't know what the mental consequences will be for the jump, but we'd be idiots not to expect them."

"Liked it better when I thought it was magic," Tamara lets us know.

I look around and see the unstated power of the Manna. Mico, formerly the most popular man on the island, is half a step above leper. His "followers" look at him longingly but keep a healthy retreat distance. Mico's missing the most important element necessary to make this work. Confidence.

"This isn't going to work."

"Why not?" he asks.

"You're talking about directing us by what you hear. No good. We've got to hear it as well. Plus, you think Tamara is a spoiled brat."

"Hey!" she snaps, but Mico doesn't object.

"She's not. She's been through more than anyone her age has a right to and she reacts to it poorly sometimes. She's also constantly managing the stray thoughts of the world. For the most part she deals with it in silence. But occasionally, yeah, she'll have a verbal outburst."

"I'll try to be more compassionate . . ."

"You're missing my point. I know where she is at all times because I can feel her neurons firing like old-school gangbangers in my head. There's an intimacy between us that's damn near cellular. Her telepathy makes it reciprocal. I can't even imagine trying to lie to her. It's this link that makes us such a problem for the Alters and others."

"You want to link him?" She finally gets it. "To . . . us?"

"For Prentis, girl. It's this or nothing," I tell her.

"Okay," Mico says after some long-thinking minutes.

As soon as Tamara links our brains, mine grows a billion dendrites just to compensate for the amount of knowledge and skill Mico has. I go down to the ground but only for a second. Tamara's brain deals with the incalculable influx far better than mine. She's used to incorporating people's thoughts. What she can't handle is the noise.

"What the fuck is so loud?" she screams with her mind, inherently threatening the sanity of the island. But Mico rushes to her, physically holding her face between his hands.

"That's the sound of the universe. We're on a planet that's spinning, orbiting a sun at hundreds of thousands of miles a second. There's bound to be some friction. It's always been there. We live in the rhythm, the breaks in the sound."

Gravitational pulses from unstable pulsars billions of light-years away make Mico's eyes throb. But he's dealt with it, with all of this, for years. His entire body is a receiving vessel. Every atom of his body is reacting to what's around him . . . or more, has the ability to shift like a stem cell. I can see my daughter's suffering and mimic Mico's ability in her. She breathes deeply and relaxes. Slightly.

"Bloody Hell!" she says with her mouth, no longer shouting. "We there yet?"

"Not by a long shot," Mico reacts. But he begins to understand. Tamara knows everything he does. What needs to happen next, how much it will hurt, the ambiguity of success, and the repercussions of failure. But still she jokes.

Mico listens. I hear. He listens, finding patterns, cadence, rhythm: the things that turn sound into music. Even being aware of all he's experiencing, I can't—couldn't ever—find what he's listening for.

"There!" he shouts. Not pointing, just bobbing his head. "I can hear it. The discord."

Tamara does her best to share the rhythm with me, but I'm useless.

"Great. How do we get there?" I ask.

Mico starts strumming on his guitar. "It's all metaphor," he tells us. "If we-us, the mover, and me—can conceive it, we can do it. Just feel it."

I see Mico clearly now—attached to everyone, feeling connected to none save a dick of a tuber god. This is the first time he's ever felt supported. A tune I'm vaguely aware of begins issuing from his guitar.

"Let your attention go. Let a second equal a minute, a millisecond, a century. Doesn't matter. It's all about the relationship between the notes."

I'm doing my best to keep my body—all our bodies—relaxed, but I've never felt gamma radiation as music in my bones before. I try to switch our respiratory systems over to autonomic control, but Tamara stops me, pointing out Mico's need to sing. Breath control. She's seeing the complex relationship between his verses and the modulation of the guitar. I flip my instincts and put all our autonomic biological impulses into our shared conscious control. It works.

Tamara has total molecular control over our bodies . . . and the world. She and I both jump with the implications, but Mico's strumming and singing bring us back into control. His mind reminds us, "You will tear yourselves apart trying to reverse all of time."

He's right. I can imagine the effect and the glorious burning of our bodies and consciousnesses. Still, all Mico does is sing. We are a three-person nervous system generating a consciousness aware of the subatomic clockwork of reality, and he's just strumming.

Tamara's annoyance at me is palpable. She thinks I should understand by now. As a clue, she co-opts my power and drains all my ear wax. Stupid and childish, but I get it. Tamara and Mico are younger than me. They naturally hear higher frequencies. I adjust my ears, and the resonance hits me. There's a pattern that, if it were replicated, if our molecules were vibrating at we'd be someplace else.

"We're not reversing the album, just popping the needle," Mico thinks at us, whatever that means. Tamara gets it. She keeps her focus on our molecules. The first shudder she attempts feels like an attack, only this intimacy gives it a suicidal tinge. Mico gets more deliberate in his strumming as a response. I check us over physically for damage and find none. No one said this would be easy.

The sky blinks blue and black. Hot air licks us then goes cold again. Something happened.

"Two days!" Mico's thought is excited and frightened. "Try extending the verse. Find the beat between then and now."

"You want to try?" Tam would be having a seizure if not for her newly efficient brain, thanks to Mico. Still, she's burning through synaptic bridges by the trillions. But I get it now. The echo of the Big Bang—each moment is just a physical expression of it. Find the cycle, and we can go anywhere. Just find the time when the echo sounded like whatever Mico is playing. Tamara's been polluted with too many sci-fi flicks. She's thinking about going backwards. The universe doesn't do that. Everything is happening, being created constantly. Yesterday didn't happen. It's happening right now. Same with tomorrow. Everything is happening, being created constantly. We hear it. We see it. We can be there.

I get it. Mico knows it. Tamara—she feels it. We travel in directions I don't have names for. And we're gone. All the while Mico plays his damn song.

Almost sounds like Marley.

ACT II

1971 London

Chapter Eight

This was the worst idea ever. I don't know how long I was out when we "landed" in the same spot we "left," but I come to before Mico and Tam. Only bit of luck thus far. They've both stopped breathing . . . and thinking. That's the first problem. Second is my skills are . . . muted. Laying hands on Tamara's heart nearly gives me an aneurysm. I'm slower with Mico's healing, and we both come through the better for it. Restarting Tam's brain is even easier. One word. "Prentis."

High-end Mods and low-level rockers walk by us on their way to the fully furnished non-torched Eel Pie Island Hotel. It's a fully functioning hotel. The place the old folks on the isle still wish it was. It's the land of pleated miniskirts and super-tight black sweaters. New rock that calls forth old blues screams nearly inarticulate from the door of the hotel. What they see, saw, of us landing obviously didn't make much of an impact. Tam still doesn't have the strength to mask us so I let the '70s progressions of cool march by us as I focus on Mico. His brain is firing on that low hum it always does, but he's barely conscious. His eyes are blinking out of sync with each other. His breath is labored then protracted. Our three-way link is broken, but I can tell the issue. He can't hear the music of his god, of the universe. He can't sonically acquire the world. He can hear, but only with his ears. Even that's not the biggest issue.

"Jaysis," Tamara keeps shouting whenever a stray racist thought goes through her. Good to know our connection is still solid.

"Block them out." I'm trying to get Mico to stand.

"It's not just the racists. There's a trace in the air, a big liminal spark. There." She points northeast. I'm playing piano with mittens on when it comes to my liminal skills, but even I feel it. Maybe liminal, but definitely powerful. Eel Pie is totally unfeasible as a base. Time to move.

Mico follows us with childlike compliance, contributing nothing save a sad and confused face. After ten minutes crossing Turkenham River Bridge, Tam "convinces" a cab to carry us after the power trail. First evidence I get of her diminished capacity is the cabbie's refusal to take us any farther into Notting Hill.

"Thought this was nothing but shops and half mill flats?" she protests as we exit the cab on to boarded-up tenement houses and the remains of blownout cars.

There's a siege mentality on these streets that I can feel. Everyone is strong in their eye checks, assessing for familiarity or threat.

"Give it forty years," I tell her.

Tam goes to her training—my training—and finds an empty flat for us. On the third floor—half a roof, really. There's no heat, but the water is still on. Abandoned mattresses smell musty but are clean enough. There are even some linens left in a closet. This was an eviction. A brutal one, if the broken dishes and blood in one of the bedrooms is any indication. It's a good location for us: at least three angles of exit if necessary, and we can see anyone coming at us. Tam gets excited for a second when she finds a rat in a cupboard. She's hoping for that half head cock of a Prentis animal. Instead it just scurries away through a hole in the wall.

I take first watch, as Tam can barely keep her eyes open. When it's my turn to rest, whispers of Samantha's voice call from some deep aquatic place. Whether it is threat or warning, dream or liminal reach, I can't say.

When I wake, Tam is sitting in a lotus position, back against a paint-chipped wall, eyes closed and mediating. I've never smelled so many different curries on Notting Hill lanes, never seen so many black faces. This flat is around the corner from a café called the Mangrove. Apparently, it's public enemy number one for London police. This is all according to my girl, picking up on stray thoughts. The tension does her no good, but she's a trooper and doesn't complain. When she speaks her voice is smooth and focused.

"I feel her . . . impact."

"Got a location?"

"Maybe if I had some help." She opens her eyes to gesture toward the man-child on the dingy mattress in the corner.

I make my way to him across the floor, reaching out with my skill. Our former intimacy still calls to me. But I've looked into his body and found nothing wrong. Behind him the early morning sun begins to warm the pavement outside.

"You ever have some coco bread, Mico? Coco bread and ginger beer is the best breakfast ever. Want to go get some?"

"You sure that's a good idea?" Tam asks, not moving. "The block is kinda hot right now."

"Me and the man can handle it, right?" I say, helping him to his feet.

On the street we're marked as strangers by our twenty-first century clothes. But even in his stupor Mico emanates a kind demeanor. Maybe it's the dreads. Little girls and boys running to school slow down around him. One even pets his hand. He smiles gently, unsure of the gesture's meaning.

I lead him through an alley to find a Caribbean market and instead find five skinheads, complete with leathers and Iron Crosses, jacking up a little black girl not yet twelve wearing a Catholic school uniform. The blades are in my hands before I think. Their desire to slice and stab infects me in one step toward the assholes. Before the second step, Mico makes his first voluntary move and grabs my wrist with epic strength. He shakes his head slowly but confidently. I don't want to fight him, but the blades do.

"Piss off, Wogs, or you'll get the same."

I split the difference of my rage and hit the yappy pale-skinned kid with the type of Staph infection that gets hospitals closed down. He falls hard, trying to spit out the epic bacteria reproducing by the billions in his throat. The others can't understand what I'm doing yet so I cause shin splints in another three. The little girl runs quick. I barely notice. The final two put the sickness puzzle together and head toward me.

I want to explode one of their hearts but only end up enflaming the lining. I overwhelm the brain of the last one with random stimulation for grand mal seizures. Then I switch their symptoms. Three times I switch them before I can hear Mico.

"Stop," he says putting his hand on my shoulder. His eyes are on the knives still in my hands. It takes too much effort to sheathe them at first. But once hidden, I return to myself.

"Why?" he asks, as I'm jacking the skinheads for cash.

"You got 1971 money?" I ask. Under his own volition Mico walks past the white spray paint in the alley wall: "Enoch for Britain." All the while, avoiding my touch.

He's coming to life slowly, in fits and starts, because of music. Desmond Dekker's "Israelites" blares from the little open-air market and Mico hums to it. As we walk back to the flat with groceries in hand, a boxy yellow Volkswagen blares a bass-heavy calypso tune from frail speakers and Mico does a quick jig. Passing the restaurant Tam told me about—the Mangrove—just as it opens, Mico stops so suddenly I get nervous.

"Prentis? Nordeen? Alters? What?"

"An ally." Then he adds, "Someone you can't stab."

"Calm down, coma boy. Who's our ally?"

"I don't know. But I know their sound."

"How do you know?"

"It's so much quieter now. The Manna. It knows I'm here, but it's not talking to me. Still it's talking. I can listen in." I pull him from the restaurant before Mico can cause a scene. Back in the flat I can see Tamara is agitated. It's not mere frustration. It's yet another goddamn problem.

"My dad is alive out there," she starts when I have piece of coco bread in my mouth.

"Not in London," I tell her softly.

"But I could find him."

"He'd be a baby."

"But I could see him."

"He would be a baby," I repeat slowly. "And what would you say?"

"You're jealous." Guess our connection isn't as strong as I thought. In our time she wouldn't have to guess what I'm feeling.

Truth is I hated the excuse for a man, her father. He was upstanding, tried to do good in the world, stood by Yasmine in a way I never could, and raised Tamara in a fashion I never could have. I called him Fish'n'Chips because that was his labor lineage. But the truth of the matter is, I'm the sad man he excused.

"Don't let your sounds cross," Mico trumpets after a strong pull off some ginger beer.

"Wot now?"

"We—here, now—are discordant enough. Making sounds only a precious few can harmonize with. Your father is an earlier resonance of you, an unrosined bow pulling against a loose string. It will cause . . . problems to speak with him."

"Now you've got something to say?" she snaps. She walks out of his eye line as he tries to apologize. "Right. I fit to blow up the universe if I stretch my legs for a bit?" I don't dare say a word until I hear the door slam downstairs.

"I feel better," Mico tells me, looking out the window into the tenement across the street.

"Yeah, she can be a handful sometimes. But you've got to realize the last time she saw Fish . . . her father, was as his car exploded."

"That's . . . I'm sorry for her loss." He turns to look at me. "But I meant here, now. I'm closer to myself. The food was a good idea. Thanks."

"Thank me by getting a bead on Prentis. I'm not a fan of 1971 London."

"Not a very good place to be a black man, is it? Has it really changed that much, though?"

"Dude, I wasn't even born in seventy-one and I'm from the States. Not that it's that much better there right now."

He nods, still in his half trance as his spindly dreads fall to his shoulders as if by command. I feel the extra part of his brain usually reserved for the Manna become active. But Mico makes a peace with his loss and keeps the search going, listening to what he can.

"There's a storm coming here, to Notting Hill. Nordeen will do his best to hide his movements in that turbulence. Prentis is too valuable an asset to leave alone. She will be with him."

"Makes sense," I say. "Burn the house down to grab the jewels is his M.O. Usually making sure someone else is holding the match."

"Question is: What are the jewels?"

"Come again?"

"You've been so focused on getting your ward back, you haven't asked why he took her in the first place." Nordeen always wanted her, since I was his pet. I never imagined her as a means to an end.

"I'll be sure to ask Nordeen when we find them."

"And then what?" He turns to face me as I snag some bread from the kitchen.

"We tool up, snatch Prentis back, and get home."

"Tamara was so convinced you wouldn't be able to fight Nordeen she took off without you. Given your intimacy, how could she be so wrong?"

"Make it plain, Mushroom Boy. What are you asking?"

"I'm asking—not stating, just asking—what's your plan when you face Nordeen? And please don't say those entropy knives. He's faced such weapons before and prevailed."

"Haven't you heard, Mico? There is no fucking plan."

Tamara worked out her vengeance on our wardrobes. She got me a deep-brown fedora, wool slacks, a button-up charcoal jacket, and a three-button, narrow-waisted navy blue vest that she commanded must never be fastened. Mico got some incredibly flared bell-bottoms; a red, black, and green net shirt; and a long Prussian blue trench coat. I'd be mad, but when she emerges from the bathroom wearing a deep red and light yellow tie-dyed ankle-length skirt and a cream-colored waist-length cashmere sweater, all I can think is how much she looks like her mother. She gives us each a new pair of Chuck Taylor low tops then surveys our wardrobe.

"Least we won't stick out." She smiles. "Now let's go find our girl, yeah?"

We cruise the neighborhood, taking turns scanning—me feeling for Nordeen or that liminal brain explosion. My girl searches minds, both happy for the relative silence her diminished capacities have given and frustrated by her lack of success. Mico listens as only he can, with his entire body. We take turns so as to not leave ourselves vulnerable to the morass of trouble on the streets.

Residents of the neighborhood meet us with guarded greetings, by and large; Mico getting dread props from younger versions of Bingy man, some of them openly smoking joints on the street. Other folks—the younger men mostly—try to approach my daughter only to find themselves inarticulate when they come close. We walk the neighborhood, up and down Westbourne Park Road, across to Talbot, over to Colville Terrace, then as far as Chepstow Crescent—like echoing bats, cycling through our powers for hours before I notice a pattern.

"We're circling the Mangrove."

"Shush, Tag. You're always hungry," Tam says, annoyed that I've interrupted her search.

"No. He's right," Mico says.

Tamara grins hard. She's scanned the restaurant. "Bloody fucking Christ on his pogo stick, wait till you see who's in there."

The restaurant is busy, clean, and loud. It's not just Caribbean folks. Some whites and South Asians relax at one of the twenty tables. It's barely big enough for all the late lunch business. I can hear fights and broken dishes coming from the kitchen behind the serving counter. But it smells fantastic. Beautiful cuts of goat and beef pass us as soon as we enter. Some people are just drinking coffee, playing cards, and talking shit under posters announcing the return of Gregory Isaacs to London. Other folks are diving into their plates, their bodies being the better for it. While the range of my liminal vision is limited, I can still focus enough to tell the nutritional and developmental differences between those Caribbean born and raised in London versus the ones recently from the home islands of Jamaica, St. Kitts, and Trinidad; their melanin counts scream for sun not filtered by London clouds and smog.

I follow Tamara's eyes to a skinny light-skinned dude with baby dreads. His face is deep in a bowl of brown fish stew. I've only seen him in pictures before, and he's younger than I think he should be. But even with none of the celebrity surrounding him, the lion-like visage can't be imitated, though many have tried. That's the tuff gong. Bob Nester Marley.

"Yup," Tamara says, picking up my thought. We start walking toward him, but Mico stops us.

"Me first. You two are too . . . just let me go first, okay?"

Tamara's still debating in her head as I sit at a newly free table. I never thought I'd see him alive. And never imagined it would be like this.

"Tell me you didn't travel back in time to smoke a joint with your reggae idol." She actually makes Mico say it before she sits across from me.

I get three orders of jerked chicken, some mannish soup, salt fish cakes, plantains stuffed with cheese and meat, and a guava shake. Tam gets the red pea soup, green banana salad, and two beef patties. I have to slow down to not empty my plates before Tam does hers. Our cute Trini waitress is already concerned.

"Think he's part of this?" Tam asks.

"What I tell you about coincidences?"

"You can usually find them up every unicorn's ass." She smiles. "But he's an ally, right Tag? I mean Marley, he's got to be one of the good ones, right?"

"You couldn't pay me enough to hurt that man." I confess, "First thing I did when I came in was scan him for cancer. Got nothing."

"Can't you make it impossible for him to get it? He's so young."

"Cancer is, at its core, just uncontained growth. I can't stop the man from growing." I wait for a second so she knows I'm not talking about Marley. "I'm sorry."

"If I were at full strength, or that damn sound would stop playing in my ears, I'd be able to feel my da, somewhere out in the world. I'd be less . . . anxious about seeing me real dad."

"Not sure I'd be able to stop myself, if your mother was alive." She knows how much I still think about Yasmine. She was the first woman I ever loved. I felt her life slip out my hands. To even mention her fouls my head.

"I don't like Samantha," Tam tells me. "Mostly 'cause I always knew she was hiding something. Wasn't expecting all this, but, still, I know she loves you. Crossed her god for you, get me? Ya think, when we get back, you might—I don't know—settle down or something?"

"I've got your back for life, Tamara. You know this."

"Idjit. I'm saying, if you wanted, I'd be ok with it. Might be nice, settling down all proper family style."

"What the hell is he talking to Marley about?" I shift the subject. She's talking about me having kids, more kids, but she can barely acknowledge I'm her father.

"Didn't even know you was a reggae fan." Tam takes pity and lets it go.

"Your mom rescued him from the Georgetown stoners for me." The pleasure-tinged pain comes back with the memory.

"Go on."

"I didn't listen to music for the longest. Wasn't part of the repertoire. When I started dating your mom she was all roots rock reggae. I just tolerated the music until she told me about his life. Then I paid attention to the lyrics. It wasn't all peace and love. It was toil and struggle. The mire of Trenchtown. She told me about him playing in Zimbabwe through tear gas. Not stopping as the rest of his crew ran off stage. I fantasized that he was like me, like us. Liminal."

"Is he?"

"Nope. More like Mico. He hears with his entire body. And something speaks through him." I almost can't help grinning. "But mostly—I hear Marley, I think of your mother."

"Anyone interested in organizing a protest in solidarity for the Mangrove 9 please come to the backroom," a sweet-tinged Jamaican accent shouts over the crowd. "A general reminder, the smoking of sensimilla or any other drugs on the property is not only illegal but puts our credibility in serious jeopardy."

More than half the restaurant moves, mostly those with coffee in front of them. Even some of the wait staff. But Marley and Mico stay seated across from each other, the tuff gong's eyes flaring up occasionally to give us the once over.

"When I was wee she used to sing 'Three Little Birds' to me," Tamara says after the bustle subsides. "I thought she made it up until I heard him sing it on an album. Strange thing about Bob Rasta? Everybody else gets the massive remix, yeah? Junior Reid, Desmond Dekker—fuck, Scratch Perry did a track with them Beastie Boys,

86

yeah? Bob Rasta don't get a lick. Not even a sample, yeah? S'like the man's . . . wots the word?"

"Inviolate. He's coming." I wipe the gravy and grin off my face. He's smaller than I expected, his energy calmer. I've only seen him facing a camera. It's a younger, far more intense Marley than Yasmine introduced me to.

"This is Robert," Mico says by way of introduction, offering a seat to the young prophet.

"You na tell me you truck with duppy-eyed gal them." Marley's voice is gruff and honey smooth at the same time. The pitch is higher than I thought it would've been.

"You sang for Duppy in the graveyard," Mico says removing all accent in his voice. "You have no fear of them."

"Word is you're the duppy conqueror, ennit?" Tam offers by way of concession. "I'm nothing but an admirer, soul rebel."

"Where ay from gal?" he asks, only half smiling but finally sitting. "'Round here, yeah?"

"Your word and your sound speak different truths. Dem word dem chop up London and U.S. slang. But it come natural on your lips. Make Rasta believe you travel far to get here."

"The call me Taggert . . ." I try to distract, offering my hand.

"This your ratchet man?" He takes my hand but looks at Mico. "Him a sad man, yanahearme? He a need new profession. Da ratchet na longer suit him, skill be damn."

"They are my . . . friends, Robert." Mico speaks before I can. "They need to hear what you have to say."

Marley sighs deep and reclines into an impossible balance on his chair, comfortable on the back two legs. It's the type of casual miracle only his kind can muster. No one else will notice it, but I scan his body to find the internal balance that matches his trick. There is none.

"This Ras Mico a true and honorable Rasta. I can tell from his word and intention. All clear. Ras Mico tell of a demon shape like a man with a animal girl in tow. I nah see her. But Ras words put on my a memory of a dream. One forgotten. It start in Kingston and my woman. Long time Obeah attempt trouble I Rasta spirit."

"Obeah?" Tam asks.

"Voodoo man," Mico hushes her.

"This happen before I came to the understanding of the imperial majesty Haile Selassie I. So I man vulnerable. The first night my queen and I spend together I ask she keep an eye out against vexation. So I say, last night the dream of that night come on me, but from then till now, I man canna remember what rassclot thing it was that vex me in that room that night. But a smile with no joy come from a shadow and take it place."

"It was a cat," I say to the surprise of the table. "An enormous black cat. Rita saw it on a windowsill in your window, then on your chest. She frightened it away."

"How the hell did you know that?" Tam demands.

"Your mom damn near recited his autobiography to me." I think to her, then address Marley. "Does that sound right? Big black cat?"

"What you doing with my woman's name on your lips, ratchet man?" There's no disguising his threat.

"Easy, Rasta," Mico interjects. "His blades are pointed at the joyless grin in the corner."

"You say it, and it reeks of truth," Marley continues softly. "But if you ask if the vision still rests in my head—nah man." I feel a buzz in the back of my throat and know Tamara has linked Mico to us again.

"Something's missing inside of him. I did a search of his mind . . ."

"You can't—" Mico starts.

"Shut it, mushroom man," I think. "Go on."

"Brain wise—like, physically—he's just fine. But psychically, mind wise, there's a pinprick of a hole right where he's describing. It's like a surgeon pulled that dream cat directly out of his head."

"Someone my ass," I think hard. "It's fucking Nordeen."

"And again I ask why?" Mico thinks. "Also a cat? Even a dream cat?"

"What you getting at?" Tamara questions. But before Mico can answer, Marley's actual voice rings through.

"What a Nordeen?"

"You heard that?" Tamara asks.

"I walk with the power of his imperial majesty, the conquering Lion of the tribe of Judah, of the lineage of Solomon and Sheba. There are no secrets in my presence, Duppy gal."

"The smiling thing in the corner, the stealer of youths and life: his name is Nordeen."

"I man nah youth, and I still breathe. So what the bloodclot thief want in my mind, ratchet man?"

"I think you're a test," I tell him.

"Test for what?" Mico asks.

"Fuck if I know. But Nordeen is a cagey fuck. I'm pretty sure he didn't kidnap Prentis and pop back in time just to snatch a tabby from Bob Rasta over here." Marley is pissed but agrees to give us some time alone at the table as we try to figure out the missing parts of this shit sandwich. Mico may hear a lot but he's fucking tone deaf when it comes to emotions. He starts us off with the most troubling possibility.

"What if Prentis isn't a hostage?" he asks.

"Fuck your face you split-cocked—"

"Hold it together, girl," I tell her.

"You said it yourself," Mico starts again. "A pinpoint absence in his memory. A dream cat. Your girl controls animals."

"Her powers don't work on dreams," I tell him.

"And you're a healer who learned how to inflict indescribable hurt under his tutelage. Isn't that exactly Nordeen's M.O.? Find a Liminal, twist them for his own purpose, then unleash them on a foreign land?"

"Doesn't matter," Tam says, coldly, calmly.

"Oh, I think it matters a great deal," Mico starts. "If she's working with Nordeen . . ."

"Then she's under some spell or shit. We knock her out and bring her home. Get her free back there."

"Lost or running," I add, "don't matter. She's clan. I—we won't let her stay under Nordeen's claws. Better to stay on task and figure out how to get to her."

Mico nods gravely then slides out to hang with Marley back at his table. As he stands I see his sense of defeat in his body language. That's the last thing we need.

"Good job on getting the Marley knowledge," I tell him. "But there's got to be more."

"How do you mean?"

"He hasn't even blown up yet. Look around. Half these people don't even know who he is. He's young, hungry, raw. And Nordeen went for his dreams. Tell me the why of it. We know that, we can figure out the next move. I simply can't believe we run into a young Marley on the streets of London by chance."

"Maybe its coincidence?"

"Ask a unicorn where the coincidence is—wanna hear what he'll say?" Tam starts.

"Enough. Go hang with your new buddy," I tell him.

Luck starts with a song. An absent forgotten tune the two singers hum together in a unity impossible to practice. Mico uses the linoleum table top for a beat as Bob Rasta starts singing an old R&B tune in a Jamaican patois. The jam meets the activists exiting the back room and they can't help but join in, giving it more of a protest feeling. Some intelligent individual gives Marley and Mico guitars and they start jamming in earnest.

Tam rocks with the music and soon the bolder of the young bucks are skanking and winding near her like peacocks trying to gain her attention. Her 21st century dancing, even muted, makes the respectable Caribbean girls in dour plaid skirts and dresses envious. They dance first in spite, then in partnership with the peacocks. In it all I see the power of Mico and Marley. They draw the crowd, bless the union of people, anoint the celebration.

Marley only has one album out in the U.K., Mico is totally unknown, but random pedestrians are flowing in, caught in the power of their jam. In under two hours, they've got the makings of a band that would put most of the London Blues-chasing rockers to shame. Three conga players, a bassist, and a flutist all get jam lessons sitting in with Mico and Marley. They could have had more adepts at their feet, but they don't instruct with words, instead with intonation, musical phrasing, and chords. Those that hear their language can jam. The rest of us can only enjoy.

I was expecting more reggae tunes, but they actually stay more toward blues. I guess American radio made it to Jamaica when Marley was growing up, because he's an easy match for Mico's wailing and complex string plucking without breaking a sweat. Occasionally Mico will drift into a Roots Manuva jam or a Fishbone riff, but then drift back to a more '60s groove. They take a break as the waiters in the restaurant give up on the capitalist enterprise and clear tables for a semi-proper dance floor. Tam points out Mico's goofy grin to me as he does a quick tuning play of "Old Man Tucker," treating his guitar like a banjo. Like a battle rap, Marley responds with a verse that holds running, Christmas, and hounds in the first verse. In the relative new silence of the Mangrove, with the night just making its appearance—sweaty Caribbeans and whites holding up the walls waiting for the danceable music to begin again—the verse makes its most disturbing impact on Mico. Unlike on all of the other Marley songs, he stumbles before he joins in. But when he does join in, there's no more powerful voice than his. It even impresses Marley; he closes his eyes and jams with his entire soul.

It's another half an hour before Mico feels comfortable enough to leave the band in Marley's hands. Reading his body tells me he's both exhausted and invigorated. It means little to Tam.

"Good on the cat guts Jah Puba, yeah? Now wot go on with tracking Prentis?" she asks while he drinks the bottle of Ting I give him.

"I . . ." He starts, then lets his downturned brow answer for him.

"A size six to the dome helpful? 'Cause I'm sure I can produce."

"Tamara! Be useful. Give him a break."

"Have you lost your bloody mind? How's this git's jam banding supposed to—"

"Okay, we'll try your idea. What was it again?"

She walks to the bathroom.

"I can't hear it all anymore, Taggert. The guitar was just a metaphor. It can't help. . ."

"Tam and I would never have gotten close to Marley. That was you. By yourself. No god, no followers, just you. You keep taking yourself out of the play, Mico, but I've been inside your head, remember? Most people clock about thirty or forty thoughts per second. Yours count in the thousands. That grand biological and psychic architecture is still in you and I tell you, I'm beginning to think all of this has less to do with me and Tamara, Prentis even, and more to do with you."

"I abandoned my god." It's hard for him to say. "I doubt it's going to provide aid now."

"You misunderstand," I say softly. "I don't think what's brought us together and sent us through time has our best interest at heart."

"Did you hear the tune Nesta played . . ."

"The one you stumbled on. Yeah. What about it?"

"It's a song that, since I was a child, scared the shit out of me."

"Hard to play?"

"No. Hard to hear. It's Robert Johnson's 'Hellhound On My Trail.' It . . . I don't have the words for it . . ."

"Shit, I probably wouldn't understand them anyway. That doesn't matter. Here's what does: those musicians. Robert Nesta Marley understands what you're thinking and playing perfectly. Work it out with them then tell us what we need to do, where we need to go. Feel me?"

He nods, takes down the rest of the Ting, and heads back to the makeshift stage like a boxer down by a few rounds. Tam comes up behind me after casually rejecting a third of the peacocks with a glance. She's looking at me like I have answers.

"Stop acting like you aren't enjoying the music," I tell her.

"Nah, mate. That's the bloody reason I jumped through space and time, to hear Jah Puba rock it out with his musical idol. Seriously, Tag, what's the play?"

"Not sure yet. But whatever it is, it's going to come from that guy or no one at all." She gains distance from me. Waiting isn't her thing.

An hour later I look on the small band, fingers near bloody, resonating with every tune. Calling this "music" elevates every other auditory experience to undeserved heights. They rock every song and make it their own, remixing and rectifying sonic defects of the original authors. I'm not surprised to see Mico in a trance, operating as a receptacle and transmitter of sound alms. Marley is almost there with him. Tam is . . . Tamara is gone. She's outside.

She's rounding the corner to St. Lukes Mews just as I get to the door. My shout isn't catching her attention. But from Powis Gardens, at the opposite end of the street, one hundred Bobbies with a clear intention of doing no good at the Mangrove move in quickly. Without Mico and Marley in there the choice would be easy. Still, I give Mico gas to pop him out of his trance, and spontaneous orgasms to the six people closest to the window, and aim toward St. Lukes Mews. If they aren't curious after that, Mico doesn't deserve the title Prophet.

I'm happy, with the knives in my hands, when I turn the corner and see Tamara gleefully walking toward a seven-foot-tall praying mantis.

"Oy!" I'm altering my mouth, throat, and tongue to whistle a tone designed to hit Tam's teen ears perfectly, as well as most animals in the vicinity. "What it do, little girl?"

"It's Prentis," she's saying with confident glee.

"Use my eyes." With thought-speed, she occupies my mind for a second and sees my truth.

"What the fuck?" she shouts, and pushes the giant insect back with the force of her rage. "How in the hell did that happen?"

"If I had to guess," I say, spinning on my heels to see another five mutant mantises—from near pale to deep green—cutting the block off, "I'd say Nordeen is involved." I advance to deal with the first mantis, confident my girl will have my back.

With a razor-sharp claw the size of a linebacker's bicep, a mantis swipes at my head. I duck under it and turn toward my right as it swipes again. I high-jump over the attacking limb and twist, aiming my entropy knife towards it. Damn things have four arms.

It strikes at me with another, and I manage a quick stab/punch. It hurts the creature but doesn't drop it. The knives want more mantis blood, so despite my best attempt to stop them, they drag me in for the kill. In launching its mostly-eye head at me and biting, the mantis loses its advantage. As it reels back to full height again I catapult my body high at its "chest" with both blades. The creature stands fully erect and the blades stab deep just below its neck. My weight and gravity do the work to release fetid entrails, organ juice, and glass-like chitin body armor. By the time my feet touch the ground, there is no more life left in the insect.

Tamara takes no joy in her work, ripping an arm off one mantis with her power and hurling it into another while dodging the curved forelegs of two attackers. I clear the space between us just as the de-limbed one bites for my girl. With a knife in its eye as an anchor, I ride it back up to a standing position as Tamara gets smart in her moves.

She takes the detritus of the block—loose stone, broken glass, metal trash cans—and sends them into her assailants at Mach 3. I play it simple and take my ridden mantis's head off with a double chop from my blades. Its body twitches and keeps striking until one of its brethren pushes its body against me, hoping to pin me against a wall. I spring off against the wall in time only by luck. I flip over the bug's body and get shoulder-to-shoulder with my girl.

The final two rub their front claws together in preparation. But rather than attack, these fuckers sprout wings and try to take to the sky.

"The hell you say!" Tam uses all her might to hold them down.

"Play it smart, girl," I bark. "Fastball special."

Battle-trained-quick, Tamara puts all her focus on one mantis—the bigger one—and grounds it. Instantly she shifts focus to me and sends me hurling into the still airborne mantis. Damn thing swats at me. I twist in the air, catching the tip of its forearm with my blade. I rebound off its back and onto a nearby fire escape. Bleeding and angry, my flying mantis comes in at full speed. I wait until I see its mandibles separate. I jump hard at it, shoving my blade deep in its maw. I hack at its thorax with my free hand while the creature falls. We land on top of its ally, now fully eviscerated by a piece of rebar and Tamara.

"Godless fucking predatory shits!" she snaps, pulling apart the giant insects with her telekinesis.

"It ain't over," I tell her as a green mist that even the most emer-ald mantis couldn't match rises off the collective cadavers. It forms a human-ish hooded figure, rounded shoulders with yellow glowing orbs looking out its shadowed head. I know it before it hisses out its first words.

"Witless healer," the Nordeen ghost mist chides me. I have to hold Tamara back.

"There's nothing here to hit," I tell her.

"The curse of your era," my old teacher says. "You are out of time. The animal totem girl is mine. Go home."

"Fuck off!" Tamara screams.

"You endanger your own daughter bringing her with you," the green mist tells me, already dissipating. "Cut your losses before you lose all you value."

I want blood—Nordeen's, mantis, it doesn't matter. I go stomping through the fog over the bodies back to All Saints Road. I've heard legends of the street battles between Black Britain and the Queen's finest. I expect it, want to slice into it. Instead I find a police force forming a respectable parameter around Mico, Marley, and a crew of other musicians, all playing on the street. The scene infuriates me.

"What, Taggert? Did they get you?" Tamara asks behind me.

I rage. I turn to see her, want to stab her pretty brown eyes out. Just like her mother. I want to slash her throat.

"It's the knives," Tamara says slowly with mouth and mind. "You would never do anything to hurt me, Tag. Fight it." Like an idiot she exposes her throat to me. No defense. Even with her power I could slice her in two before she could think—bathe the blades in liminal blood. What wouldn't they be able to cut then? The liminal blood of my daughter. With filicide, what could stop me?

The idea breaks me. Terrifies me. Not Tamara. Not her. I sheathe the blades and put them in my jacket.

"What happened to you two?" Mico asks after he's able to clear himself from his adoring crowd.

"As usual, Tag to the rescue is all. Wot go on here, Jah Puba? Gotta draw a crowd no matter what you do?"

"It was either that or watch a riot jump off," he says. "But I think I figured out where Prentis is."

"Go on then."

"Mississippi."

"'Cause that makes sense how?"

"Around June 1938."

We both walk away from him.

Chapter Nine

"Who the bloody hell is Robert Johnson and what the fuck does he have to do with Prentis?" Back at the flat Tamara starts barking at the crooner. She's tired. After the mantises, I had her wipe Marley, et al's memory of us just be sure we don't fuck time streams or anything, despite Mico's assurance we can't. My girl did it, but combined with the combat, she can't help but be cranky.

"He's a famous Blues man I've been obsessed with since I was a child," Mico says, trying not to patronize her.

"This a Mico Magical Music Tour through time now?"

"No, but your father was right—"

"Don't call him that!"

"Fine then. Taggert was right. All of this is about . . . Prentis is just a means to an end. She's a tool . . ."

"A weapon." My voice lets me know how tired I am.

"Exactly. A weapon to be used against me," he confesses.

"High opinion of yourself, ya git. Tag and I squared off against giant praying mantises while you were performing your proto-Live Aid. They didn't seem concerned about you."

"The Alters . . . Nordeen knows a direct physical attack wouldn't equal much against me. But an assault that combined the psychic, the physical, and the spiritual? Without the aid of the Manna? That would destroy me."

"Marley's cat." I'm beginning to understand. "The dream of a demon animal isn't something you can sing away, is it?"

"Exactly. It hits on the very level of my abilities."

"'Fuck does it even mean?" Tamara demands, putting herself on the floor mattress. "Dream of a demon anything?"

"People like Robert Nesta Marley—like Mico—their dreams and lives hold potency and power. What's more they pull the attention of the Nordeens of this world," I tell her. I'm fighting to keep my eyes open.

"It's more than that," Mico interrupts. He's up on the broken-tiled kitchen counter looking down at us as though he were about to give a lesson. Where did that discombobulated mess of a man I led to food this morning go? Tamara goes quiet for a moment.

"The music you heard, the way we got here, can sound like noise. But if you can hear with it, jam with it, let it own you, then it gives you power, the ability to speak with reality. Marley speaks—spoke—that reality clearly, deliberately. His acumen with it is almost as good as mine . . . was."

"Wot reality? The man died of cancer too damn young. Why didn't he hear that song?"

"Because he focused on representing the black human life as a full spiritual life instead of focusing on his own life. But you're right, he missed a beat. It's hard work, constantly listening to the universe. I think Robert Johnson did an even poorer job of manipulating the forces he had access to."

"Meaning what?" And there goes her accent.

"Meaning what Marley kept inside in a dream, Robert Johnson sang out loud and hard. Nesta and I both heard it on the recording of the man. A compilation of his work was released recently—relatively I mean. But it was recorded in 1937. Less than a year later, Johnson died."

"I'm not a bluesman, but even I've heard the legend. He sang at the crossroads and sold his soul," I tell him.

"This isn't that," Mico corrects. "Robert Johnson never really settled down; he travelled a haphazard path his entire life. Other musicians would be playing with him on the street and he'd just walk away, disappear for weeks. They said it was like he was always running."

"From what?" my girl asks.

"That song Nesta and I chanted back at the Mangrove—"

"Which bloody one?"

"'Hellhounds on my Trail.'" My voice is almost a whisper. "You're saying they were real? The hellhounds?"

"Real enough for Nordeen to grab the way he grabbed the demon cat from Marley's dream," Mico wants to confirm. "I think."

"Well, get right certain before you asks me to do that time travel fucking jump thing again, yeah?" She almost shoves him with her power as she stands and heads to the door. Then to me, "Giant mantises I can deal with. This guy . . ."

"It might not be safe," Mico warns, but I'm depleted, almost asleep. Besides, she's already out the door.

"It's an unsafe world she's grown up in. She's fine."

"I thought it was just loyalty between you two," he starts. "But it's more. It's love."

I tell him to keep watch just before I lose consciousness.

My body sleeps, but my mind races. Long tan roads choke the only image of Robert Johnson I've seen with dust. He's wearing a poorly made, ill-fitting pinstripe suit with a matching small-brimmed hat. The dust storm behind him masks hungry canine teeth, Nordeen eyes, and a version of Prentis that's more savage than I've ever seen her. I want to help, let him know.

"Taggert!" I hear Samantha behind my non-existent body and feel her bruised, beaten, and burned. But I don't see her.

"What happened?" I yell. She can't hear me. I know this smell. It's burning flesh.

"They've already won here." She doesn't hear me. "You've got to stop them before they get here."

"I'm trying! We're trying!"

"If . . . if you can't . . . don't come back." The dust-bowl storm comes from nowhere and blankets my every sense.

I'm awake before I know I've slept. My girl lays out on her mattress comatose, belly down, drooling. The Dread crooner stares out the window catching what passes for London morning sun on his face. I don't need to see him to tell he hasn't slept, but it's the loneliness that catches me by surprise. I keep expecting to see an unnaturally friendly smoke surrounding him, or an adoring clan. Last night, watching Mico jam with Marley in front of a crowds I saw a glimmer of the man in his element. It was Eel Pie Island Mico. Did he know all he'd be giving up by travelling with us?

"All quiet?" I hear him hum a low tune. A protective spell if ever there was one. True spells aren't spoken, they're sung.

"As quiet as London ever gets." He forces a smile. "Tamara told me the details of your mantis fight when she got back. No wonder you were so tired. She brought back some food for you."

I grab some spiced bread and ice-cold sorro from the dilapidated fridge and head back to Mico.

"It wasn't just the bugs," I confess. "The knives are . . . I guess it's what A.C. said. They are heavier than I thought they'd be."

"He makes it look so easy," Mico says, surprised I remember the wind man but not looking at me. "That sword of his, those guns. They would crush most others."

"How does he not . . ." I'm useless for words.

"His god gives him strength."

"Fat lot of good that does me." I almost laugh until Mico turns and eyelocks me. Not aggressive, just serious.

"There are no atheists in foxholes. Sometimes you've got to be in the middle of a war to find your god."

"You calling this a war?"

"The opening volleys, if nothing else" he says slowly. "The last echoes of the first creation are dying out. The birth gasps of the Big Bang are fading. Either we, as a creation, start to unite to build a rejoining chorus of life together, or whatever entropy engine Kothar is coming up with will mute the very resonance of life."

"Kothar. That's the Alter specifically tasked to the Manna?"

"To me, actually. He's been . . . after me since long before I knew what I was supposed to do." I hear it then. Fear in his voice. Honestly, I don't care.

"I just want to find Prentis."

"And that's the problem." The Manna said something similar, and it confused me then. This time I kind of understand, but I don't have time for it. I drain the sorro.

"My girl can't do the time warp again."

"What?"

"Look at us. We're all diminished. I thought it was the knives at first. But even your singing voice isn't as strong as it was in our time. And Tam never sleeps like that. She's in a near coma. When was the last time you've seen a psychic rest so completely? It's not exhaustion; it's weakness. And we both know she did most of the heavy lifting popping the needle on the cosmic record player or whatever."

"We can try . . ."

"So we can be weakened even more? Don't be the git she thinks you are. You've got to find another way."

"The only other way—" He snaps at me, then calms himself. "It leaves me near powerless once we get to Johnson's time."

"Afraid we'll let you fall?" Tam says from her bed, not moving. I felt her consciousness ping me for details of our conversation the second she woke. "Thought we was a team."

"You don't understand," he protests. "The only way this is possible is because we're crossing the Atlantic to visit another person of African descent. A long blood debt is owed that will allow our spirits, and by extension our bodies, to travel across space and time."

"Makes about as much sense as you usually do," Tamara says, sitting up.

"But the blood debt was from enslaved Africans, and the last thing they want us to do is go to the Americas."

Some songs are more powerful past the sight of land. That's what Mico says. We ferry out as far as we can, then Tamara carries us in the air, close enough to the ocean to have high waves touch our feet. We're flying in the middle of the damn ocean. I'm about to shout at Mico for making her do the heavy lifting again until he starts wailing.

It's impossibly loud. His throat can't possibly be making that sound, and his soul . . . it can't contain that much suffering, right? His listening body has transformed into a projecting vessel. It's such a lurid enunciation Tam's concentration almost slips. I grab her hand off instinct. She's happier for it.

Mico's soul lamentation doesn't stop, but he looks at me desperately. I grab his hand and feel the drain that sustaining the notes puts on him. I'm thankful for the truck full of food I devoured before we left, as I heal and replenish them at the same time: two people, at once, these two that require not only focus but sensitivity. When I close my eyes, I feel more than wind rush past us.

It's like the wind boy's travel, only harsher. I feel resistance, but light changes to night and back to day in minutes. We're travelling through time. On the strength of Mico's wailing.

"He's playing the record backwards," Tamara shouts over the resistance.

"I'm not," Mico mind-barks at us, not missing a note in his singing. "I'm begging the souls of the dead to let us pass. Now be quiet!"

"Well hurry it up, yeah? I'm good for short bursts. This long-term push isn't my forte."

I shush and heal her at the same time. Mico rejoins his own voice, almost singing backup for his own tune. I keep my eyes open this time. Watching the strain on both their bodies. We might not make it. I don't even know what that would mean. Stranded somewhere between 1971 and the 1930s . . . in the middle of the Atlantic. That would be the best-case scenario. I look behind us, into the past, and see a shape descend under the waves.

Tamara catches my tension, but I get her to stay on task. I don't want to disturb Mico. But whatever it is, is coming. It's following us, through space and time. And it's fast. The shadow of a giant fish is directly under us. Tam and Mico are too focused on the movement to notice. I make the decision in a second, before Tam can read it and stop me. I put Mico's hand in my daughters and let them both go.

The shark jumps just as I fall from Tam's levitation bubble. The blades are in my hand and scraping the back of the prehistoric hammerhead shark's back just as I create gills in my neck and ankles. I hear Tam scream my name as I go underwater.

Chapter Ten

This fucker will not have me for lunch. The blades agree with me. I beef up my arms and legs then insulate with a thin layer of fat just below my skin while the wounded hammerhead circles, trying to intimidate me. Worse than him have tried.

I do the reticulating lens trick just as the side-eyed fish makes his approach. I dive quicker than it can clear the space between us, then reverse course even quicker, angling up, right at its soft underbelly. The blades scream for its blood.

We pop up to the surface, actually catching air. In midair I flip the sixteen-foot beast and hack away, slicing, stabbing, ripping. If I had any compassion left in me, I'd be finding a way to end this thing's life instead of making sashimi. I want to expose all of its organs to the sun. In the seven seconds it takes to hit the water, I've turned the shark into chum. Shit.

"God damn it Taggert!" Tam yells at me from a hovering distance overhead. "More coming!"

I go underwater to see eighty-five different varieties of sharks that make my first look like a guppy. All of them coming my way. I'm about to swim for them when Tamara pulls me from the water.

"I got this!" I drop my gills and underwater body modifications.

"Shut your gob and listen, yeah?"

"They're not normal sharks," Mico says, his acoustic time-travel-projected voice totally halted. "They're the ones that fed off the Africans."

"Slave trade's been over for a while," Tam chides.

"These are the nightmare sharks of the Africans that survived. These sharks have developed a taste for . . ."

"Dark meat," I hiss. "Black blood. I got it. It's another trap courtesy of Nordeen and Prentis. The plan is the same. Chop, kill, and keep moving."

Mico's smarter in a fight than I give him credit for. He has Tam drop him underwater briefly in a bubble of air. Whatever he's singing is enough to get some of the sharks to surface. With the girl's help I make shark-fin soup of the thirty-yard radius around us. Tam gets the singer out of the water just as the nightmare sharks begin feeding on each other. They may like the taste of Africans, but all species learn to kill each other first.

Only the most horrible, tenacious ones break the surface and aim for us. I'm ready, but Tam takes the bull sharks and the great white on a tour of the sky, tossing them fifty feet in the air. When she misses a black-tipped shark coming up from the rear, I find my moment to shout.

"Look out!" She drops me from shock, and I kick off Mico's arm to meet the beast in midair. I rake its right gill while stabbing its eye. Fucker rolls its body on me as we hit the ocean surface. And me without my body mods. I make more chum meal out of the black-tip shark while holding my breath. But a bite hold on my leg drags me down. I exhale all my bodily toxins through the wound and the leviathan gags. I dive deeper, raking and scraping anything moving my way. I'm maximizing the oxygen, in my body but I'm using it up too quickly. I should grow gills again, something to keep me alive. But all I want to do is slash and kill.

I scream underwater for more, want them to come to me, when I feel a strong tug skyward. I hold fast to the tail of one shark already half gutted and continue to punch-stab at it when I get air. My screams are born from joy as Tam deposits me on the wooden deck of a ship, shark in hand, still punching. Why would I ever stop slicing? Tamara screams in my head to get my attention.

"It's dead, Tag!"

I feel cheated. It didn't suffer as much as I wanted. I need more flesh to stab. Not Tam. That much I hold on to. But Mico. I would like to see the color of his blood. I start toward him but the body of a girl—rail thin, Asian eyes, and milky chocolate skin—gets in the way. She moves . . . I've seen this movement before, like a deadly ballerina.

"Remember yourself," I hear Tamara shout. I leap for Mico. My jaw, throat, my biceps, and the back of my neck are all struck at the same time. All I can see is black.

The ebb and flow of the tide pull me from sleep more than Mico's mournful hymn. But the shock of being dry and not floating shoots me up. I'm on a boat. An old-world, three-sail Chinese junk, to be precise. It's impossible for its well-worn planks and sun-touched sails to be weathering the mountain-sized waves. But the ship is here and so am I. So are the entropy blades, resting by my feet.

"Get those things off my deck," a disembodied voice says from the rudder wheel. "And do right with them or I'll kick you back to sleep." It's the chocolate girl, in baggy sweat pants, a black T-shirt, an open gray vest, and a bandanna over her head, not covering a thigh-length queue. At least that's what my normal eyes see. My liminal sight can't find her. Mico sits above her, chanting against the waves in the crow's nest.

Collecting the blades, I have a second to wonder where Tamara is before she comes up from below deck and smacks me from port to stern with one telekinetically assisted blow. I knew she'd get me back.

"Asshole!" she shouts. I don't bother trying to get up.

"Go easy. All that hack and slash tired me out."

"You trying to die?!"

"Of course not. What else was I going to do?"

"How about not dive into spirit-shark-infested waters? Those knives are fucking with your brain."

"And if it wasn't for them you'd be dead right now," I tell her softly as I stand, cautiously. "Look, they're a pain in the ass, super dangerous, and not good for me in any way, shape, or form. Agreed. But they cut through giant bugs and the sharks. They can probably slice through Alters as well. We're getting weaker the longer this journey goes. We need all the help we can get."

"I need you." For a second I want to call her daughter.

"So does Prentis. So I'll use whatever weaponry, tools, prayers, and allies I can get my hands on. To hell with the cost. Speaking of which, where the hell are we and who's the quick kick?"

I guess Mico realized his channeling through time wasn't going to work. So he changed his tune when I went underwater. He called out a name that his pet Alter gave him before we left. Chabi, her name is. This is her boat. The *Mansai*. The spirits of the Africans took a brief pause when she showed up, and all the remaining sharks ran. But now the Africans started up again, whipping at the entire ship in the form of a perfect storm. It was taking all of Mico's singing and Chabi's piloting to avoid capsizing. For the first time since we started this trek, Tam and I are just passengers.

Time means nothing here, so I don't know how long we're waiting as the girl with no body I can see and the troubadour steer this strange fight for us. But when the ship does a full one-eighty under the influence of a forty-foot wave, Tamara gets nervous. The air is thick with wisps of smoke masquerading as bodies, screaming in tears, moaning, and pleading as terrified dead Africans whip around us.

"Long as they've been dead, ya think these slaves would've calmed down a bit," she tries to joke.

"They're not slaves," I tell her, touching her back gently. "They're mothers and fathers. Bankers and bums. They're blacksmiths and professors. You think of slaves, you think picking cotton and driving mules. But it's more than that. These spirits, even if they made it across, they never would've been slaves because they knew where they came from. But their children, and by extension us—you and me—we will always be slave children."

It's not that the waves abate as much as they collect at the aft of the twenty-five-foot ship, while the winds threaten at the starboard side of the majestically faded red and black sails. Mico takes a moment in the relative calm in his song-fight to attend to us.

"We're in deep now, yeah?" my girl asks, fear tinging her voice for the first time.

"We ain't out of it yet. That's for damn sure," the bodiless girl speaks—in a language I don't know but understand perfectly.

"Chabi is doing a lot, but she's not . . . substantial enough to take on all the spirits by herself."

"We can help, right?" Tam asks.

"There are no bodies or minds for you to work on," Mico apologizes. Then she does it. Tamara, scrapper supreme, bar-none shit-talker, the original posh turned chav, kills me with her eyes: she looks at me, either sea mist or the beginning of tears in her deep browns, and silently begs for a solution, like I'm a teacher with the right answer waiting to see if she'll get it. I can't disappoint her.

"This is just the eye of the storm," the captain says in that non-voice. "It's about to be a shit storm up in here. Might want to go below deck."

"You!" I shout over the rising winds at Mico. "You're a body I can work on."

"This isn't about strength or brains," he says.

"Your flesh, brain cells, it's all putty in my hands, boy!" I shout at him. "That's got to count for something. This is your world not mine. Think! Stop singing and think for a second. What calms spirits down?"

"Sacrifice," Chabi tells us as she starts walking a large circle on deck. It's that same patient, deliberate movement that goes everywhere and nowhere at once. Where the hell have I seen this? I pull a bewildered Tam out the way as the girl who doesn't speak with her mouth begins moving with marked purpose. The ship responds to her body, swaying the way she does, thrashing at her command, arching in time with her slightest leg movement. When the wind and waves start again for real, we are protected. Barely.

"They need a sacrifice?" I turn toward Mico. "They can have me."

"Fuck they can!" my daughter shouts.

"A sacrifice must be clean." Mico tries to be gentle about it. "They don't want to add to their numbers."

"What do they want, Mico?" I'm shouting.

We're knocked—I'm knocked—off my feet and have to grip the side rigging to keep from going over. A wave the size of a building wants to snap the *Mansai* in two. Impossibly the ship arches backward until the wave is about to break, then it turns and rides the crest as I lash myself to the perimeter. We ride the impossible wave like a surfboard, hitting it head on and watching in silent panic as uncounted African spirits scream at us from the water to turn back. Tam's doing slightly better, but that's only because she's straining her telekinesis. Mico is battered but still on board. It lasts forever before the dark sky above gets farther away and we descend back to a relative normal height. Waves ahead promise more of the same. Mico sings at the helm while Chabi continues to dance, spar with nothing save stray spirits.

"You're not appeasing them. Your girl can't fight them all. We've got to negotiate. Come on, Mico! What do they want?"

"They don't want to be forgotten," Tamara whispers in our minds. She's levitating in a lotus position in the middle of the *Mansai*, working her best to commune with the spirits. Her words mean nothing to me, but the crooner gets something out of it. He runs to the highest mast and starts shimmying to its top. Tamara gives him a telekinetic boost as I boost his and my ATP levels and fat-burning muscle and climb up behind him.

He howls. Inarticulate, devoid of all music. It's a primal scream heard above wave, storm, and thunder. They all silence for him. That's when he speaks.

"How can I forget you? You are written on our skin. You want me to carry you? Fine. You will be my strength." He turns to me in the crow's nest. "The cross sections of the slave ships. Have you seen them?" I've never heard him out of breath, hoarse before.

Tam shoves the familiar vision in my head. I nod.

"I need that image on my arm." He pushes me. "Permanent. Not just pigment, you understand? I need it to be part of me."

I start raising skin, pigment, scar tissue and bacteria to craft a relief of pain and suffering on the crooner's arm. Despite the swaying of the time-ocean and our mutual panic, he doesn't move. The time pressure is a distraction. The threat of the next spirit wave wrestles with my focus. But I breathe deep and stay attentive, creating as beautiful a representation of objectification as I can manage. Each huddled shade has a space representing eyes and a mouth. Each body is proportional. Each chain linking hands to feet or neck is damn near photorealistic. I spend myself utterly on his tattoo, linking nerve endings with each millimeter of arm space. It takes Tam to keep me standing with a telekinetic push.

"Done," I tell him.

"I hope so," Mico answers me, then barks back to the sky. He lifts his right arm—my new work—unceremoniously to the sky. "Come! Come to your child and know you will never be forgotten."

They come by the thousands, tens of thousands. Half eaten, fully whole, children, men, old and young women. They come flying into his arm, each electrifying Mico, making him a bit stronger, each taking a little power from the storm and donating to Mico's ready physical frame. Each is a little easier to take. He doesn't scream out as they come but damned if he doesn't want to. It's just him and me in the crows' nest. I hold him close, not daring to heal any part of him. This is the sacrifice. He can hear the fits and starts of the universe and

111

dance but the suffering of the Africans almost breaks him. Almost. When Mico is saturated he pulls his arm back to his body, cradling it as though injured. There are still spirits in the wind, but significantly less.

"The resistance is passable," the captain says from below—and all around us. He doesn't complain, but I help Mico down the crow's nest anyway.

"All right then?" my girl asks him.

"I have the middle passage's nameless souls on my arm. I don't think I'll ever be okay again."

ACT III

1938 Mississippi

Chapter Eleven

An hour equates to a year on this ship, if Chabi is to be believed. That means we've got a day and a half until we get to New Orleans, which is the closest she'll get to land. Of course, when I ask her why her mouth doesn't move when she speaks all I get is a wry smile. Tamara wants me to thank the non-existent gods we're alive and let it go. Mico's been recovering below deck ever since his new mark.

In the travel spirit version of night—a quickly creeping darkening of everything from the west, followed almost immediately by a warming glow rising from the east—I hear a rare joy: Tamara chatting it up with Chabi. Grinning in her voice. I used to think my daughter was a lesbian. She still may be. She's attracted to powerful women. The only times she ever fought with Prentis was when the animal girl refused to acknowledge her own power. Tam has no tolerance for weak women. This Chabi doesn't know how to spell "weak." I stare off the starboard deck to give them a modicum of privacy as they chat and spar.

"Broke all the bones of one of them," the captain says, doing her strange boat kata.

"I threw one of them into the ocean," Tam counters, levitating above the deck in a lotus position.

"Which one?"

"Poppy, they call her. She was knocking around in my head like she had the right to be there."

"Little rat-tooth wench? More skin and bones than meat?" The ship goes still and rigid as she stops moving.

"That's the one."

"Next time you see that one rip her limbs the fuck off and burn her eye sockets out for me, would you?"

"Easy enough favor. What she mean to you, then?"

"Sooner all of them go back to whatever shadowy abyss of uncreation they got shit out of, the better we'll all be." The ship starts moving again, slowly, calmly. "That one, though, she took an innocent I knew. A friend. I don't have a lot of those."

"Sorry for your loss, yeah? But you've got two new friends, if that helps at all."

"Careful with that word. Circles you travelling in now, it could get you killed."

"Think I don't know that? Me and the old man are going through time, scrapping with nightmare beasties and angry African ghosts off the strength of loyalty to a friend. I know the value of friendship and what it costs. You pulled my . . . Taggert out of harm's way. Even saved him from himself with bomb-ass kicks to the head, yeah? Debts owed, the way I see it."

"Mico introduce you to an Alter he keeps on a leash? Goes by Narayana?"

"Yeah." The hesitation in her voice is born from a recognition. I have to look over the deck to see it. Chabi's c-steps, her imaginary steps, her entire system of occupying space, it's the same as Narayana's.

"Next time you see him, you let him know Chabi's coming for his ass."

"Understood."

"Cool. Now let me show you some moves."

✳

They train until Tamara almost passes out. They could almost be sisters. Chabi is older, has a bit more swagger, and is obviously more deadly. But I stop the associations there. Something is wrong in Chabi. Precious few are immune to my liminal sight. And those that are usually walk too close to death for the healer spirit in me to be comfortable around. But Tam was right. This Chabi is closer to friend than enemy and no friend of the Alters. I feel a Liminality about her.

In the quickened morning, Tamara sleeps as Mico rises. In the inbetween time, Chabi and I keep our distance. She gets a look of disdain every time my hands go near the entropy knives. I breathe slightly easier when I see the American coast.

Real ships appear ghostlike as we pass them in a perpetual mist of spirit. As Mico comes to my side of the *Mansai* to survey the southern leg of our journey, I examine my handiwork on his inner arm.

"It's . . . animated," I tell him.

"Believe me, I know. We've been working a peace treaty that would put the Hague to shame." He strokes the living tattoo reverently. "Lots of different tribes and languages forced together in this small place."

"Luckily you're used to having millions chattering in your dome." He nods, still stroking his arm. I point to Chabi. "What is she?"

"She's a mystery."

"No shit. That's why I'm asking."

"To me as much as you. We were desperate. You were underwater for a long time. Longer than you realize, I think. Before we left, Narayana said that if I were to need help and I was near water to call out her name. Chabi. He didn't tell me what would happen or who she was."

"You don't know her?"

117

"Look, I'm dealing with a lot here right now. My recall isn't perfect. She looks . . . familiar, but I can't place from where. Her name is like a fading whisper . . ."

"Shut it, singer. How do you know she's an ally for real and not an Alter trick?"

"I called out in the spirit of friendship."

"Sounds pretty desperate."

"We're in the foxholes, Taggert. Might be time to choose your God."

By the time we reach Georgia, Tamara is up and mimicking Chabi's katas to near perfection. By Florida she adds her own telekinetic flair to them. It almost feels like a party when Chabi brings up an ancient boombox from below deck and starts rocking the old-school drum and bass. Mico can't help but add his own mouth and body percussion. His voice has more resonance now, supported by the spirits. Tamara thinks of inviting me to the dance party-training session, but I'm still not trusted by the captain. I can't read her body, so I don't trust her either. But I do respect her martial skills, the moves she's sharing with Tam. Chabi knows bodies from the outside in, while I feel them from the inside out. It's natural we don't get along, I guess.

Heading west and hugging the coast, we all feel the slipping of time easing.

Distant ships are beginning to hail us. Real currents and tides are affecting the *Mansai*, and Chabi's back at the rudder wheel.

"Sure you don't want to come with us?" Tamara asks Chabi.

"Personally, I'd love to. But it's not in the cards." There's genuine sadness in her voice as we angle into the booming port of New Orleans. The huge steamers and docked ferry boats barely seem to notice us.

"My debt to you . . . ," Mico starts, losing his thick coat against the real-world early evening mugginess of the Port.

". . . will be repaid someday," the captain says, eyelocking him hard before he walks the gangway to dry land. She nods hard to Tam, who does the same. I try to avoid conversation, but she's not having it.

"You know what I am," she tells me, quiet enough to keep from Tamara.

"Dead," I confirm. "You and this boat are bound together. One. It's why you can't get off."

"Mico's way too trusting," she says, nodding at my guess. "Your daughter is too green. Don't let them end up like me. You see an Alter, you destroy an Alter right away. No talk, no negotiations."

"That's the plan. As soon as we get Prentis back."

"And if it's either or? 'Cause I might have been offered the same deal as your Prentis. But I got lucky and chose death."

"You know the value of family."

"And that's how they keep fucking us over."

Tamara understands the full implications of Chabi waving good-bye to us from deck as the *Mansai* slips back into the spirit fog. She does her best not to cry, but her moist face reflects the moonlight perfectly just for a second as we turn to face our first gulps of 1938 air.

Chapter Twelve

"I thought slavery was over by now," Tamara breathes out slowly from the back seat of our pilfered 1937 powder-blue Dusenberg. She was fine to steal it, along with suitable clothes, but she'll be damned if she was willing to figure out the clutch, let alone the choke. Mico was smart enough to give her the backseat so she could catch some rest, but ever since we hit the Mississippi line she's been complaining about the shocks and every other damn thing she can think of. The spit-boil heat and dust of these Depression-era roads is not helping.

"They're not slaves," Mico says, catching her reference: a dispossessed black family of eight with all manner of cloth bundles for luggage. They make their way up a shale dirt road, and we all feel guilty zipping by them. All their clothes are repurposed flour sacks and gingham, and they all have holes in them. "The Depression is in full swing here, and it was always worse for black people . . ."

"They freed us but didn't really have an idea about how to pay for what they took from us," I interrupt.

"What 'us'?" she asks.

"My people are from this land. That means half of your people are from here. Us."

"All right Mister Black Nationalistic," Tam mocks after Mico directs me down a red clay dirt road. "Still, someone might want to go back there and tell those suffering bastards they're free. I mean, it's miserable with heat in here and I can only imagine what they're feeling out in the sun."

"That's not the job." I sigh. The break in the afternoon heat gives the promise of evening air soon. This Flintstones engine and I could both deal with a temperature drop.

"Right. We're following the cosmic Barry White's cosmic dream to Robert Johnson in order for what now?" Tam asks, leaning forward from her seat.

"What'd I say the first twenty-five times you asked?"

"You'd tell me when we got there." I'm happy to let my silence be the end of it, but Mico's been getting anxious since we left the *Mansai* half a day ago.

"Is this some grand strategy you two have trained in?" He sighs out hard. "No plans, just run headlong into danger?"

"You ever been punched in the face?"

"Let me! Let me!" Tamara bounces.

"I boxed as a kid." Mico ignores her.

"Good. Then maybe you've heard the expression 'Everybody's got a plan until they get punched in the face.'"

"Can't say I have."

"Wanna feel it?"

"Quiet, Tam. Listen, man, you want plans and strategies? Go find a soldier or a general or a hacker. I've got to diagnose, see what we're dealing with, before I can even imagine talking plans."

"The real question is you, ennit?" Tam says with a light smack to the back of his head. "You know how the old man and I get down. When it's time to turn on the whip-ass I'm on hot, and Tag is cold as cancer. Where are you?"

"You're asking if I'm willing to fight?"

"More like can ya,' cause for real fam, I'm trying to call up a time I've seen you throw a punch, and I'm coming up with nothing."

"Not all fights require fists."

"Yeah, well this one probably will." She keeps pushing. "That Chabi girl, yeah? She was dropping serious knowledge about the Alters. Where and how to hit them, how to smash their bones and make 'em so they don't heal back. And where was you?"

"Mollifying the rageful spirits that threatened to tear the ship apart." He turns to face her. Angry.

"Girl's got a point," I say, turning back on to a state road.

"You're questioning my ability as well?"

"Not your will and drive, but yeah, your ability. Every conflict we've been in, you've called on allies. Outnumbered or outpowered your opponent. Well, your only allies in this time are sitting in the car right next to you. And we'd be idiots not to test your jaw. The Alters send Nordeen to kidnap our girl and collect musical night-mares specifically to launch at you. Now I've been punched in the face my whole life. It's okay. I heal. Sometimes I think Tam likes to get knocked down just so she can get back up. You prepared to stand up on your own? No god, no kin, no clan to help? Plus the weight of the countless souls on your arm?"

"I don't know if I'll . . . win," he says just before I turn the car and we hit newly paved road. "But I promise the both of you and Pren-tis I won't stop fighting until the Alters are done . . . or I am." I risk eyes off the road to survey Mico in the fading amber light of the sun. I'm expecting a wary but resolute face. But he's calm, placid. Almost peaceful. I believe him.

Ten miles outside of Edgerton, Mississippi, we stop at the first gas station I've seen in hours. It rests to the side of a stately, small three-story livery draped in decaying clinging vines and yellow moss. A groggy, skinny white-boy attendant who will need braces by this time next year saunters toward the car.

"Make us white," I tell Tamara.

"You make us white. It's fucking degrading, ennit?"

"So is lynching. No way three niggers in 1938 can afford this ride. Now do it!"

"Racist," she says quickly, then gives the gas jerk a vision of us as eccentric New Orleans proto-hippies.

"Boy, where can I find some of that negra Mississippi Delta blues music I keep hearing so much about?" I say, doing my best white-man-from-Louisiana accent.

"Well, sir. Big Sally's ain't but four miles up the road. Saw Son House there last year 'fore he found religion. Boy go by Skip James had a house band up there not three weeks earlier."

"Expert in the field," I say, handing him a stolen silver dollar.

Big Sally's is half kitchen, half bar, all moonshine speakeasy; a decaying small house next to an unused acre-and-a-half field. I can smell the unrefined distillate as we pull off the freeway by the wooden makeshift sign and into the cleared dirt parking lot just outside the two-story sheet-metal-roofed building. The four sets of five columns that line the porch are ornate in their bases, making me think this used to be more than a juke joint. There's even a babbling creek behind it somewhere—I can hear but feel more, as it hydrates the dry-as-sin air. This was a rich plantation owners' guest house at some point. But those days are over for this spot. We park next to cars far older and more rusted than ours, as well as the odd donkey and horse. Huge, drooping trees shade them all, forming a semicircle around the little cleared area.

Low fashion as she is, Tam knew she had to rock a dress and so she's slid into a blue-gray number with lots of give in the legs and a close hold on her near non-existent hips. Mico took the slacks with suspenders and the yellow button up she gave him with thanks. But she had to clown him with an almost zoot-suit jacket to go with it. I'd told him to take the shoulder pads off in the car. I'm fine with overalls and a red thermal top. The straw hat I scored on my own.

Early in the evening, the stomping tunes from inside only threaten full volume. The bullfrogs still win the sonic contest out here. But there's a body cacophony raging inside. Bones compacted by labor, far denser than I'm used to, melanin counts much higher as well. Half of them are infested with hookworms and damn near every penis inside is infected with some STD we've eradicated in modern times. But most importantly, they're all human.

I should've had Tam mask us before we walked in. Between Mico's dreads and Tamara's comparatively light skin tone we might as well have walked in naked. The two guitar pickers and piano player on stage doing their version of "Don't Start Me Talking" make it all about Tamara as she makes her way to the bar, unperturbed by the turned heads.

"Heard you pour the best applejack in the country." Tam slings her accent and pilfered knowledge at the thick-necked Big Sally behind the counter.

"Where you from, girl?" Sally almost laughs at Tam as she sets each of us up with our own mini mason jar with dust-chafed hands.

"Back East, Ma'am." Mico steps in. Sally's not feeling Tam's lack of manners. "We were sent by the W.P.A. to work on classes in reading and writing at the library. Figured we'd come down early and get with some of this legendary music of yours."

"Nigga, you lie worse than you comb yo hair!" She says it with a voice that dwarfs the stage act. "Dis what the devil look like if a Bible was a comb." Everyone starts laughing.

"He one of them Garveyites," I say, tapping my empty jar for a refill. That alone gets her notice. This applejack is definitely more jack than apple. "He read something said the Israelite preachers of old never cut they hair. He figure he gonna try it."

"Umm-hmm," she says, filling my jug, peeping my eyes and then my hands. "And what about you, dead eyes? You ain't look like you following no God 'cept death. You trying to stab a nigga in here tonight?"

"We ain't here for trouble." I scan her quick, making sure I didn't miss any liminality. Nope, she's just a smart black business owner in the South. She knows how to read people.

"Only time I know that ain't true is when I hear it. Dolla buys your first round, fried chicken dinner come with hush puppies, fried tomatoes, and gravy. That fifty cent."

"Got rooms to let?"

"Only one. Dollar for two of you. One of the men can sleep in the car. This ain't no freak house."

"My daughter ain't a freak," I say calmly, laying out the only comprehensible thing about us: twenty dollars in 1938 money. "We'll take four dinners, another round, and a night's lodging, at least."

She's about to fight me on it when Tamara's voice starts coming from the piano at the side of the makeshift stage.

"She ain't getting paid for that," Big Sally barks.

"I didn't even know she could sing." But I know the song.

"Some father."

In our early days together, Tam, Prentis, and I all slept in the same room, under pressure from the girl who couldn't have her pack of snakes, rats, dogs, and cats around her at all times anymore. My version of a lullaby, really an absent tune I hummed more than sang, was Tom Waits's Christmas card from a hooker in Minneapolis. The tragic mythomanical tune always calls to my most sympathetic parts. But I've never heard it in a woman's voice. Didn't even know Tam had a woman's voice when she wanted. Didn't know she could play the piano. I almost tear up at the delicate beauty of an open secret between us.

"Been shielding that from you for months now." After appropriate applause and props, she smiles when she comes back to the table Mico secured for us.

"Why?" I ask, wiping chicken grease from my mouth.

"Birthday gift." She's fully aware of my discomfort with her display, but she doesn't care. One of the guitar players is launching into "Lord I Just Can't Keep From Crying" with a voice weaker than Blind Willie Johnson's.

"Everyone's going to be talking about you and that song," Mico says.

"My plan," Tam says with a fried tomato in her mouth. "We've been chasing them for literally seventy years now. And they let us, yeah. I mean it's obvious they wanted us here. Why else send the sharks if not to let us know we're on the right track? So let's get the show on the road. We're here. Let's get the whole county, state, whatever to be talking about the hot chick, the old man, and the snake-headed weirdo hanging at Big Sally's."

"But you're introducing a song into the universe before it was intended," Mico says.

"Come on," I tell him. "Even that hellhounds song has antecedents somewhere. When you jammed with Marley you didn't play anything recorded past 1971? It's music, man, no one owns it; it flows. You know that. Besides, Nordeen's already done worse. Trust. It's a good plan, girl. Get on it, Mico. Jam with the band. Make Big Sally's the place to be. That's what you do, right? Rock it hard enough and your boy Robert Johnson will come, as well as Nordeen and whoever is backing his play. We'll be in wait for whichever comes first."

"And Prentis," Tamara adds.

"Exactly."

"You want to square off here? It's . . . it's not near any powerful ley lines, it's . . . you want to take them on at a juke joint?"

"Notice the floor? Freshly mopped but still stained with blood. What is this? A Thursday? That means someone got stabbed on a Wednesday. It's not yet six o'clock and already they've got an opening act for a bigger band. This place will be jumping come Saturday night. And with the liquor Big Miss in the back pours, there's gonna be some more blood spilt. This isn't a juke joint, this is a bucket of blood. And when you've got blood, passion, and music—well, you've got power."

I share the vague outlines of a plan that might give us the upper hand, just this once. I make it sound like there's more to it than there is. They nod like I'm deep. I lie and say I'm going to check the perimeter as one of the guitar players busts out a harmonica for "Pony Blues." As soon as I hit the porch, I know who I'll see.

With the sun down, the baking earth smell fades into the scent background with the uniformity of cicada mating chirps. I try to make it a calming meditation as Nordeen strides calmly through the nearby unkempt field. The same dark hood keeps all but his yellow glowing eyes and occasional red-sparked mouth shrouded.

"That's close enough." I'm fighting pulling the blades.

"As if you could stop me," he tells me in the old Berber tongue he first taught me. He doesn't stop advancing, so I descend from the porch to meet him in the parking lot.

"I mean it, Nordeen," I tell him in English, one of the blades now in my hand. He stops hard. A near-caution takes his body. "Where's Prentis?"

"You know exactly where she is. I took one. I left you your blood. You should have accepted your loss and kept—"

"You don't get to tell me what to do anymore. And you don't get to kidnap my kids!"

"How much of an idiot are you? You think I took your charge out of choice?"

"Don't pawn this off on the Alters!"

"I told you from the beginning we all serve someone. They've wanted someone like her since before I even found you."

"But why serve them at all? Entropy? How can you get behind entropy?"

"I acknowledge the futility of doing any less." He tries to circle toward Big Sally's, but I side step so he has to rotate towards the parked cars. "Besides, you've met the root god's champion. Does he seem a savior of humanity to you?"

"He sings a good enough song. What do you want here?" I ask harshly, scanning for Mico and Tamara.

"They sent me to keep you fixed," he tells me, stroking the Duesenberg. "But I've come to give you an out. Take your child and return to your time. Enjoy what relative peace you can muster and leave Mico to his fate."

"This just coming from the kindness of your heart?" I ask, trying to stay focused on him as he slips in and out of the wooded shade, and not the deep green glow coming from our ride. "Or do we pose a problem for you?"

"I'd sup your soul in a bowl made from your daughter's skull," he tells me in a casual voice lacking everything but conviction. "But for the fact that I once had hopes for you to sit by my side—"

"Oh, shut it, old man," I shout, feeling rage from the blades calling to me. "I've heard enough of your manipulations to know when you're lying. I'm not leaving—we're not leaving without Prentis. Bring her back if you want us to leave."

"Out of time, weakened, a child, and an excommunicated prophet as your only allies. Do you truly believe you've got bargaining power?"

"I've got you here talking to me," I smile.

"No." His sparky mouth smiles wider. "We've got you here."

The Duesenberg explodes with a deafening roar. I only take my eyes off him for a second, but Nordeen is gone.

Tam and Mico are the first ones out the door, followed by an angry shotgun-wielding Big Sally.

"What I tell you?!" she says, pointing at me. "These niggas ain't nothing but trouble."

Chapter Thirteen

Mico had to grind hard to keep Big Sally from kicking us out. I missed most of the negotiations, being outside manning the fire brigade. I boosted all the volunteers' dopamine and endorphin levels and made their bodies toxic to hookworms. They came back to the juke joint in better health than when they left. By the time I walk in, Mico's pimp-slapping a banjo with one hand and using a bottle to slide notes with his other hand. Somehow he's got the whole crowd—some eighty-plus farmers, drivers, maids, hustlers, servants, skinflints—all stomping and clapping in unison.

"Wot was that then?" my daughter demands. I give her the quick and dirty. She fumes in silence then punches me playfully. "Look at you, backing down your custom-made boogeyman."

"Ready to do the same?" I'm checking her eyes for confidence.

"You think that Poppy chick will be here?" she says almost below the music.

"Makes sense. She was the only one at Nordeen's."

"Bitch took me down with a whisper."

"You tossed her into an ocean."

"You got her to stop that chaos yapping." Tam moves to the bar and orders a shot with a double knock on the wood.

"What? You want a pep talk?" I ask after we both take a shot.

"Fuck off! I need to . . . practice."

"That's my girl." I catch myself, but she lets it go. "Me too. We keep an eye on this madness, sleep as much as we can. Tomorrow morning we get at it."

"What about the blues brother?" she asks through another wave of applause.

"Shit. He's getting stronger by the minute."

"Can't right study you two." Big Sally, drunk, one breast almost free of its oppressive stained yellow captor, shotgun in hand, greets us as we descend the stairs just after seven. "But that snake-headed monkey up there can blow down them Jericho walls."

"I'll be sure to pass that along." Tam laughs.

"Hey!" The heavy woman points her shotgun at us like a giant finger. "'Sploding car is about as much weirdness I'm fitting to tolerate, long green or not, understand?"

"What other weirdness is there?" I ask, chilling Tam out with a hand on her back and healing up some of Sally's drunkenness.

"Not three days ago heard about ol' gal over there in Natchez. Middle of town, bright as day, they swear a hundred or so rats attack an old girl. Just her and her alone."

"She live?" Tam asks.

"Ever seen a barn rat tear through an egg? Times that by a hundred and ask that question again." Sally puts her shotgun down and aims for water. "Two things I don't allow in my business. Rats and white folks."

"Racist," Tam says under her breath. Then to me, "Prentis has never used her animals to kill in her life. What's that psycho done to her?"

"Same thing he did to me for years. And I survived. She's stronger than me. Come on. Time to train."

We find a small tributary of the Mississippi river about fifteen miles from Big Sally's. In our time it's probably a pool of toxic sludge, but in 1938 it's teeming with life and tastes almost sweet. We build a silent meditation the whole run there, me spot-healing anyone I feel in a fifteen-yard radius while Tam snips visions from their eyes or sounds from their ears. We stay to the weeds in part because no one jogs yet but also to track animals, checking for signs of Prentis's influence. Every squirrel, coyote, rabbit, and hawk seems natural as we go by. By the time we hit the lake, we're both in our liminality.

We don't speak in this state. She doesn't have to read my mind to know the only place it's safe to practice is away from prying eyes. We know each other's instincts on a physical level, and so it's no surprise when she follows my dive into the lake. On instinct I grow two complex gill-filtering systems, complete with a gall bladder–like organ to hold the gunk I can't make use of. Tamara makes another telekinetic bubble, much like the one that held us up over the Atlantic, but smaller and pulling in oxygen from the surface. Through it I hear her say, "Bring it."

I grow the lenses as I pull the entropy knives and beef up my arms and legs. Tam's only tell, licking her lips, gives me my impetus to attack. The worse menstruation cramps ever double her over as I launch myself despite the eighty feet between us. Halfway across she focuses through the pain and crunches my spine like an annoying piece of cartilage between teeth. I switch all my pain receptors to cortisol inhibitors and stretch my spine back out, not stopping. Neither is she.

No lens could clear my eyes of all the sludge and muck she's pulling up from the bottom of the lake. It only took five seconds to get to where she was, but she's gone. Before I can scan for her I'm tagged hard from behind. Feels like a fire-hose flow. I go with it, curling into a ball, then spin to the direction it's coming from. I get hit with a harder flow from my right, at my knees. I hold on to the branch of an old fallen tree to keep low. I clear my mind so she can't track me, and wait. Smart moves on my girl's part. My tactic would be to rain down as much damage in the murky area as possible. Not Tam. She likes getting close.

Oxygen-filled lungs tell me her strategy. She went for air before she descended into the muck. She swims right by me. I nerve-strike her leg and watch her concentration go. I'm on her quick, python-wrapping my legs around her stomach. I sheathe one knife and come around her throat with it. I feel the blade's excitement.

Tam pushes both her forearms against my super-yoked, knife-wielding bicep. Her panic is just fueling the blade. I have to beef up my arms even more when she adds telekinesis to her strength. The blade wants to see what Tamara's body will look like without a head. I have to think back at it.

"One drop of her blood and I'll leave both of you at the bottom of this lake. No flesh for you to pierce, no blood to wet you, I swear to you, blade. You are mine. I am not yours." Instantly the soul weight of the blades lightens. I think it's happening physically until I realize it's Tam. She shoots both of us out of the lake and high into the air with the force of a cannon. In the instant it takes me to switch back to an air-breather, she lands seven telekinetically aided shots to my face, ribs, and groin—no doubt learned from Chabi. I fall to the lake beach hard on my back. Tamara lands efficiently, her knee half a millimeter from my throat.

"Not bad," I tell her. Not moving.

"Bull." She falls to my side, observing the same sky. "I panicked."

"Should've kept higher ground. Taken your time with pot shots until you hit my location. Then you bring the hammer."

"I know. How the was the blade work?"

"We've come to an accord for now. But you've got to learn to work with the resources you've got. That was the point of going to the water . . ."

"Shut up," she tells me as she sits up on her elbows. Across the lake a brown rabbit sits at the bank, head half-cocked, staring at us in that Prentis-touched way.

"Oy!" Tam barks to the rabbit. "Ya hear me, gal?"

"Prentis," I join in. "Time to come home."

I think the rabbit is about to leave when it turns around. Instead it stands on its rear paws to meet a speckled coyote with the same Prentis head cock. I try to say something, but the attack is over before I realize there's nothing to say. The coyote savages the rabbit with a near-human maliciousness. There is no desire to eat in it. The bite is designed only to kill and discard. The mangy coyote stares at us, blood and fur stuck to its mouth, then ambles into the lake with deadly intent.

"She doesn't . . ." I hear the tears in Tam's voice. "She knows that coyote can't hurt us."

"It's already dead." I pull her up to her feet and turn my back on the scenario. "It's a message from the other side. Hunter and hunted are both damned."

The southern heat dries our clothes as we walk slowly back to the gas station that pointed us to Big Sally's. In full afternoon light we see more houses, people, and shops. Sheet metal is a luxury here. Most buildings are haphazard constructions made from repurposed ancient local wood. The difference between shacks and houses in this town seems to be porches and a floor made from anything other than dirt. And again, the damn hookworms. Barefoot or not, rich and old, mostly black but even the white people are teeming with worms.

At the general store-gas station I grab cans of sardines, rock candy, five pickles, half a pecan pie, six apples, two quarts of milk, two cokes, and half a pound of sliced salted beef. I expect some smart-alec comment from Tam, but she stays quiet even as she works the subtle trick of convincing the shopkeeper our money is dry and the amount of food I buy is normal.

We post up on the porch separating the entrance to the shop and the gas station. I'm deep into the pie when she finally speaks.

"You've been okay to kill Prentis from jump." It's her resignation, not the words, that hits me.

"Fuck you," I say. "I'm not here to kill our girl."

"I know that, but if it comes to that . . ."

"It won't."

"What do you always say? 'No need to plan for the best.' I know you don't want it, but if it comes to it you wouldn't want that blood on my hands and you wouldn't trust Mico to do it."

"Stop it, girl."

"You're misunderstanding me, Taggert . . . Dad. I'm not mad. I get it. You would rather take her out than see her in Nordeen's hands. I didn't, couldn't see that before the rabbit and the—" I numb her vocal cords so she can stop talking. I drain her ears of wax so she can fully hear me. Then I speak.

"I'm not killing Prentis. You aren't killing Prentis. She's not dying."

"Wot you gonna do when she comes for you?" she asks, using her mind. But before I can answer, we both notice a guitar picking that sounds a lot like Mico's. The voice, deeper, calmer, obviously isn't. I lean over the porch to see all the children of town and some of the teenagers shaking and bopping to a little black shiny man with a wry smile in a worn brown pinstripe suit.

"No fucking way," Tam says in my mind. I reactivate her vocal cords, and she croaks out, "Can't be no Robert Johnson."

"Looks like your plan was right," I tell her. "See, keep hitting bad luck and you're bound to get some good. That's why we never stop, Tamara, get it? Even when you don't have a plan, no idea what's to do next, when you've been punched in the face by the bigger and better more times than you can count, you stay fighting. Stay in the game, yeah?"

"Nordeen teach you that?"

"I wish," I say. "My brother." She goes silent. I don't talk about him much on purpose. "He was one of us. First Liminal I ever knew. And he was a savage. I at least had him as a model. He came first and had no support. Fuck, I'm still making excuses for his shit."

"Family." Tam consoles me, taking a genuine interest, trying not to be distracted by the crowd of folks flowing around the corner for Johnson.

"Yeah, family. Big brother. Stronger than me, better than me. I didn't even know how to hurt people with my power back then. But I beefed up and beat him into a drooling incontinent mess of a retard."

"Jaysis, Tag. Guess he wasn't stronger after all."

"He was. Smarter as well. But I got him by surprise, and once I started wailing on him I didn't stop. Whatever he gave I took and kept coming. That's how I've been training you and . . . Prentis. In every fight . . . Fuck it, life is gonna punch you in the face hard. I know it already has, but there'll be more. I could've focused on teaching you how to avoid blows, but . . ."

"They ain't us." I hear her pride.

"Yeah, kid. That ain't us. We're counter-punchers. We see the left coming, we throw the hard overhand right first."

"Eat a shot to give five." She nods, loving learning a new part of me.

"And make them count. Tamara, when I was your age I was still playing at normal. I was stabbing myself in the hand to see how quick I'd heal. You've travelled through time, faced off against Entropy Gods and ridden on a ghost ship. All for the love of fam. You know how many people would be broken by now?"

"Aww. You saying you're proud of me, Taggert?"

"I'm telling you I love you, little girl." She clears the table and hugs my head before I have a chance to stand.

"Pardon, ya'll," Johnson's voice calls to us from the street. "I'm sorely hungry and'd 'preciate any bit of Christian kindness you might could muster."

"You that Robert Johnson plays 'Pony Blues' better than Son House?" Tam asks, not bothering to let me go.

"According to some pretty lady. Build my strength up with a slice of that salt meat and maybe you judge yourself." He smiles and tips his hat.

"Better than that, let's head over to Big Sally's to get you a proper meal. Plus there's someone I want you to meet."

Chapter Fourteen

Just when I can see the burnt-out remains of our Duesenberg, waves of deep-space cold emanate from a human form in Big Sally's. I shut my scan down hard. Not wanting to risk pinging Mico, I give Tam the high sign and she loses herself with Johnson in tow. He's happy enough to walk off with "the pretty little yellow girl" he's been hitting on for the entire walk. Crossing the abandoned field that borders Sally's gives me time to prepare. To relax.

Sitting alone in the middle of Big Sally's empty joint, a male version of the rat-bitch Poppy sits in a cream-colored, narrow-shouldered suit complete with matching riding boots. If Sally's right hand isn't on her shotgun behind the counter, then she's not the moonshiner her liver tells me she is. Her bloodshot brown eyes blame me as I clear the span from the door to the Alter's field of vision. Confusion inhibits his ability to sip from the Mason jar in front of him.

"What are you?" It's the voice of privilege, elitism, and excess that issues forth from that impossibly small mouth. I'm compelled to respond just to stop it from talking again.

"You don't know?" It's all I can do to not scream at it. It's using a lighter version of the same chaos voice that broke my girl in Morocco. It takes a long drag of the air.

"I smell my sister on you, but an older version of her. You're obviously a Liminal, but I've killed all the black Liminals in a 500-mile radius." I have to deaden Sally's arm so she doesn't raise her shotgun.

"Guess the better question then is who are you?" I say, quicker than I want to, and sit down across from him.

"I am Poppy. Complementary twin of the Rat Queen. I kill niggers."

"That so?" My liminality builds calf muscle on instinct, wanting me to run.

"Oh yes. It's a great time to kill niggers. No one cares. No one who matters, anyway. I've killed over one hundred and fifty niggers from Carolina to Texas in the past four years. Drowning, lynching, shooting, strangling—all of it. Any way a body can be maimed or tortured, I've tried. The murders themselves are inconsequential, you understand. They were just models for others. A 'how-to guide,' if you will. Naturally it's better for humans to come to entropy through their own steam. But of course, they need prompting. That's why I haven't included my plague in the body count."

"What plague?"

"The hookworms. Didn't my sister tell you? No doubt she's jealous. The Spanish flu was hers. An admirable attempt to be sure . . ."

"Spanish flu wiped out 5% of the human population." I'm trying not to launch myself at it. There's something off about this male Poppy. It spits into its empty glass, and a hair-thin, translucent, writhing wisp of a worm appears.

"Exactly. Wiped them out. Killed them completely. And if there's one thing the human creature knows how to do, it's reproduce. All she did was thin the herd. No, my hookworms weaken the entire herd. They kill during birth—mother and child—leaving a deep malaise in their wake. But even better, they slow the growth of the brain and mind. They're not deadly, you see, but they aid in the entropy of the human animal."

"I am Taggert. I am a healer." I beg for the blades in my hands to be quick enough to catch whatever fresh hell this perversion is about to throw at me. Its mockery of eyes blink hard. Something has changed for it.

"You are not under my sister's sway," it says slowly. It's pissed.

138

"I helped toss your twat sister in the ocean," I say with a hungry blade under the table. The hookworm in the glass feeds off his rage, growing from a few centimeters to a nine-inch writhing anathema in a matter of seconds.

"That never happened." His voice alone is cripplingly loud. Its emotion, so potent with power, is barely comprehensible.

"But it will." Ice speaks from the doorway with a British accent. Another Alter. Older, dressed in khaki safari shorts, complete with a circular medium-brimmed hat.

"Kothar, is this Liminal yours, or am I allowed to destroy it?" Poppy asks, not bothering to look behind him.

"It is not mine, but it serves my purpose. Even now it has delivered the champion of the Manna to us." He strides through the room with large steps, surveying everything with disgust.

"Don't tell me that fat, bloated, ignorant heifer is what you've spent your existence preparing for." Poppy finally looks away from me and turns to Sally.

"Fuck you, cracker," she shouts back before I can deaden her vocal cords. In a second her body is teeming with hookworms. She begins to double over in pain. I numb her agony, make her body inhospitable to the worms. In another second she's shitting and vomiting them out violently. It's embarrassing for the woman, but at least she'll live. Kothar smiles like someone told him a bad joke.

"That human has nothing to do with my plans or the Manna. The healer is from another time. He's searching for something an agent of your sister stole from him."

"Give her back." I keep my eyes on Poppy, who hasn't bothered to stand.

"Fair trade, Ibn Nordeen. The vassal for the animal girl . . ."

"Why are you conducting your business without regard to my concerns in my domain?" Poppy shouts.

". . . and your brat delivered to Poppy for a much-deserved thrashing," Kothar says to me casually. Speaking to Poppy, his chill goes to a deep freeze. "It was the child of this one that embarrassed your other half. But in general your concerns are of little relevance to the Uncreated Cold Dark that we all serve. Remember that, Rat King, when you speak to me, or I'll return you to the Still and Quiet."

For once I'm happy the blades are in my hand. When Poppy stands abruptly, I snap into a combative stance. It laughs at my reaction and slides to Kothar's side, a clear half a foot shorter and significantly less bulky.

"Yours is the way of the Gelid Stagnancy," Poppy says, performing a conciliatory bow before the bigger . . . thing. The older Alter approaches me, dodging bloodstains deftly.

"A smart leader knows when to admit defeat, when to retreat," Kothar says gently next to my ear as he pulls on his stray chin hairs. "But you are not smart, Taggert. I have watched you for years. I know you. You will fight hard for what you've already lost."

"Then what are you waiting for? If you know so much, if I'm so dumb, let's get it on. Two of you and one of me. Odds are with you," I say, totally unsure of what I'll do if he takes me up on it.

"This isn't about you, failed healer. You are the least of the Liminals. I can destroy you in my sleep. I want the vassal. Give me the vassal in twenty-four hours or I bathe in the animal girl's blood."

I'm too frightened to say anything as they walk out. Instead I run to Sally to check on her. She's stronger than she looks, doubled over behind the bar.

"You okay?" I ask.

"Got any Christian in them heathen eyes of yours?" she says, mortified by the smell of her evacuated bowels.

"Nope," I tell her while helping her up.

"Good. Then you send them bastards to your heathen god for justice. You some kind of hoodoo man?"

"Some kind." She pushes me away as soon as she can stand. I go back to the still squirming worm in the glass and kill it with another glass.

"You got trick enough to handle them two?" She pours whiskey—real brown liquor aged from a barrel—for the both of us.

"Don't know for sure. I'll tell you this for free, Sally, your help would be appreciated."

Tam did it right and kept Mico from Big Sally's. He'd gone up the creek behind Sally's to "collect more songs," whatever the hell that means. Tamara caught sight of him half a mile upcreek and contented the two musicians with each other's company until I signaled the okay to come back. Johnson seemed comfortable with dodging unknown powers for his own reasons. Wish they'd come back with better news.

"They already took the hellhounds," Mico tells me after I brief him on my double-Alter confrontation. He doesn't ask why I'm mopping up vomit and shit with white vinegar. He's scared, so I can't be.

"They beat us to Johnson?"

"He had a dream similar to Nesta's a few days ago. When he sings 'Hellhound on my Trail' there's no spirit in it anymore. The thing I heard in the recording—it's not there."

"So we can't turn the hellhounds on Nordeen and them."

"And they'll be coming at us this time tomorrow."

"Wouldn't put too much stock in that timetable. Classic bait and switch. They'll try to catch us with our pants down."

"What are we going to do?" he almost shouts. "Half the plan is null and void. Poppy is bad enough. You've witnessed its power before. And Kothar. You don't know Kothar. Alters don't have an organizational structure to speak of, very little unity. They detract from each other and humanity equally. But none of them even think of touching Kothar. He's their Alpha male. I should have seen him as the architect of all of this from the beginning. Do you get it, Taggert? He has one purpose, he exists for one reason only. To end me. What are we going to do?"

"We're not going to run." I stop moping and enunciate each word. "There are no allies coming to the rescue. No ancient god is going to save our bacon. It's just us. You, me, and Tamara. Remember? Badness is coming. There's going to be a fight. One side is going to win, the other is going to lose. Time to sack up and tool up, Mico. Time to risk getting punched in the face."

I see a thousand 'what ifs' play their infinity games on his face. Then the steely reserve he wore in singing down angry spirits, hateful cops, and the souls of black folks: he gets it.

After the mopping, I pour shots for all of us and listen as Robert Johnson and Mico jam on what can only be called murder music. If Mico is a banjo beater, Robert Johnson is a guitar domestic abuser. He plucks strings, pops them, stomps the ground, chokes the neck of his guitar. His technique usually comes after a lifetime of proficiency. But he's not even thirty years old. He sweats and stares, impressed at Mico's near howls on stage. But Johnson is strumming with a purpose as well. To an empty gin joint, save for me and Tam.

"Round two," she says after I tell her about boy Poppy.

"Talk about racist." I laugh.

"Fucking disgusting is what he is. Hookworms? He's a hookworm god?"

"Should've known something was off back in Biya. He's going to be yours. Don't touch him. But if you do, get to me right away. I'll purge you."

"Right."

"I'm not playing, little girl . . ."

"Something I've said make you think I am?" Not much little girl left in her. "Like hell I'm going into battle holding my daddy's hand." She musses my hair a bit before standing. She's going outside to train. When Mico and Johnson take a break, the blues legend takes her seat.

"Hear tell tonight might get interesting."

"If you want to undersell it."

"Glad to help, you understand. That boy Mico make a convincing case. Thing is, I ain't much of a fighter. . . ."

"I'm not asking you to raise a fist. Just keep jamming with Mr. Banjo over there until you can't. After that, probably best to start running." Johnson nods and takes a few sips of a fresh pour of whiskey before he speaks again.

"This about that dream I had the other night?"

"And that hellhounds song you put down last year."

"Ain't nothing but my version of a Skip James—"

"It's all lost on me, blues man. This is what I know: you made something—said something that has an impact long after you die. It's about running, knowing running isn't gonna do you any good. I know the feeling. And so do millions of others. Just like I know that sometimes you've got to stop running and face whatever it is that's on your trail."

Fatigue spoke through me as Robert Johnson listened, so I went and did my best to get some sleep in the loft bedroom. It's not the heat, the impending fight, or the music downstairs that keep my mind conscious as my body rests. It's Samantha.

She feels farther away than ever in my sleep, but still I see her withered, beaten, an amorphous shadow on a red and black horizon. From that unreasonable distance—land, sea, and years away—I know she sees me. I start to scream her name, but she shakes her head vigorously. Something, someone is tormenting her, but she stays silent. She falls hard, crumpled in pain. Her spirit horizon shape forms eyes like pin lights and looks silence into my body. She can't have me saying a word.

Whatever her tormentor is, I can't see it, can't feel it. All I see are its effects on Samantha. Its invisible hand rakes her face. Silhouetted skin gives way to unseen teeth. It's killing her. She's dying. I feel it from here. I beef up my legs. I'll jump that telescopic distance. But she screams.

"You've got to win!"

I wake to a room tossed by a Titan. I couldn't have done all this damage in my sleep. These aren't nightmares. Whatever's happening back home is real enough to impact the world here.

"Nigga, what'd you do to my guest room?" Sally's slapping feet herald her coming long before she pushes the door open.

"You really want to know?"

"Knew I shoulda kept going to church," she says, leaving the doorway. "Come on downstairs if you want some food."

It's not just for me. Big Sally got in the kitchen and made a feast for all of us, Robert Johnson, her three bartenders, six members of the house band, and some hungry children outside.

"Do what you did to me, dead eyes," Sally tells me, referring to the worms, as I watch Mico and Johnson arrange the tables of the juke joint into one long table. "But take some of the heat off it."

"Already done. Gotta say you're taking all this in stride, lady."

"Sheeit. My mama scrapped with night doctors and voodoo priestesses since I was little. Big powers like fucking with little niggers." She points to Johnson. "Shit, just ask that nigga right there. If he ain't a dock for demon interest, don't know who is."

"This starts going down, you get everybody you can across that back creek to safety, yeah?"

"Long as you promise to slice that one put worms in me." She laughs.

"Not a problem," I lie.

Cheese grits, clabbered milk, chicken and rabbit stew, hush puppies, fried okra, tomatoes, turnips, baked sweet potatoes and apples, candied yams, collard and mustard greens, five large lake trout breaded, six broiled chickens, and for me and mine a lamb and beef steak each. Glass steins of black beer and bottles of whiskey and moonshine border each setting.

"Far as last meals go, we could do worse, yeah?" Tam says as she sits down next to me. Somewhere she found gear more suited to her style of combat. Thin black pants, hobo-like fingerless gloves, and a black pullover too tight for the times. She's braided her hair back like Chabi's into one mid-back-length queue. When it taps the back of her chair I hear the razor trapped in the small tuft at the end. I nod softly. Her hand is hot and sweaty when I take it in mine. I remind her to breathe deep by example. She takes it in and relaxes just a bit. In this small moment she reminds me of Yasmine.

"Looka here!" Big Sally barks directly over me from the head of her table. "Ya'll ain't need to know why you're getting fed so good. Best ya'll just give thanks and move on. But I'll say this. Tonight you might see some stuff you wish you didn't. That moment come, best to run. After this, y'all won't want for strength."

Quizzical looks over take the assembled. It's obvious Sally's never been much for public speaking. Mico's kindness doesn't allow him to watch anyone stand alone. Almost as if planned, Johnson begins his open D style tuning by the stage as Mico's slight vibrato puts everyone in mind of preaching from the other end of the table.

"I've travelled . . . well, a long way to get here with folks that started as strangers. We've been assailed by flesh and spirit to the point where, I'll confess, I'd lost my way. The hard times aren't over, but my strength has returned. I got my second wind. See, my god abandoned me, and like a fool I kept my knees bent. It took the strong hands of my friends to help me stand like a man . . . maybe for the first time. I'll tell you this truth so that you understand and carry it with you all your days. So that you tell your children and their children: your god may abandon you, you may be lost in place and time. But your friends, your true friends, will never abandon you. And that's the only power you need."

A host of "hallelujahs" and "amens" go up before he sits back down. Even Tam is grinning a little. She takes a pull of beer, then muses over the dinner din. "Maybe we's ain't such a bad influence after all, right, Tag?"

"Right, kid," I tell her, cutting into a juicy lamb steak.

Last night's jam session was crap compared to what Johnson and Mico are laying down. Even the drummer got off the stage, ashamed of not being able to keep up with the poly rhythm of Mico's foot stomps and Johnson's guitar slaps. Well-seasoned horn players and a bassist hold up the wall with their instruments securely fastened and hidden as the onstage duo works their way through the catalogs of Skip James, Lonnie Johnson, Texas Alexander, and Buddie Petit; if Sally is to be believed. No less than three hundred black bodies are rocking, stomping, swaying, sometimes crying in time with the music, begging Mico to "Go on!," demanding Johnson "Watch out now!" One intrepid young harmonica boy almost gets beaten by the crowd when he tries to blow with the duo. But Mico even makes that part of the act, rescuing the kid's instrument and humming four ruckus bars of joy into it.

"Thanks for the help, kid." Mico grins as he throws it back to the kid in the crowd. Everyone laughs. Everyone but Robert Johnson.

As is his custom, he plays standing with his back to the crowd, swaying vigorously to the music. But there's menace in his sway. Johnson does to the crowd's soul what Mico does for their bodies. Johnson is the pied piper in here, infusing his chords with a dark and deep magic. Unconsciously. Leaning against the back bar with Sally, I'm as entranced as everyone else. Until the rodents begin to pour in.

Chapter Fifteen

Ten rats for every human flood Big Sally's in seconds from the doors to
the rafters, the window, the floor boards. Big rats, nasty and cruel with
overgrown buck teeth desperate for flesh and claws designed to scoop
eyes from sockets. Each with a slightly cocked head. Prentis rats.

What weapons that exist in the speakeasy—straight razors,
switch blades, small caliber pistols, and bats—are quickly produced.
But Mico is faster still.

He plays an unknowable chord on the banjo, and all the rats
freeze in mid-motion.

"Ain't y'all heard? This is our house tonight!' he howls. The rats
respond by filing up to the stage and sitting in rapt attention. I catch
Tam out the corner of my eye: prepared, but not tense, a stark con-
trast to the crowd—all of whom have gone from revelry, to horror, to
fascination in under a minute. Mico makes it all part of his show, not
missing a beat where even Robert Johnson has stumbled.

"Out. Go out, you plague-infested carrion-eaters. And tell your
masters I'm coming."

This is not the type of fight I like. Straight ahead, outgunned and
outnumbered. Kothar in his safari gear waits outside of Big Sally's

casually, a near-snarling Poppy to one side of him, an obviously dazed but still rabid Prentis on the other, with Nordeen damn near holding her leash. Folks that don't listen to Sally's yelling follow Mico and the rats out the front door. He stands on the porch, eyelocked on Kothar. The heat between them is enough to make most get in their cars, if they can manage, or just run. I take my place by Mico's side. Tam is the last person out, making her entrance with murder in her eyes. Together we all descend the stairs.

"You've given every which way but straight ahead to get at me, Kothar," Mico says. "Are your imaginary balls retreating into your body in this zero hour?"

"You think I'm afraid of you? Cut off from your god with rogue Liminals by your side, and out of time? You're a loose end. Nothing more."

"A loose end you haven't been able to clip," I tell him, stepping forward. "Enough of the lip-flapping. Prentis, time to come home, love."

"The animal totem is ours," Poppy hisses. Tam's locked in. I boost her system by 50% and give her a natural endorphin high as a go sign.

"Wanker," she whispers. I don't know how she's able to move so quickly but in the ninety feet between us she manages to break the sound barrier. The telekinetic punch she throws misses Poppy's jaw by millimeters, but when you've got a sonic boom behind you, close is good enough. He goes flying back. Miles. She takes half a second to admire her handiwork then flies off after him.

I cram every bit of the Dame's brain cancer into Nordeen. It's like shoving a filet mignon down a swirly straw. It'll only incapacitate him for a few minutes. I'm banking on that time. But from above, in the shadows of the trees, a beast darker than a black hole leaps, separating me from Mico. Big Sally's flickering porch light is the only thing that helps me see it clearly: a black lion, a perversion of the Conquering Lion of Judah depicted on the Ethiopian flag. The cat they wrestled from Marley's dream. It's the size of a pony.

"Come on, Prentis," I beg, circling, keeping the lion's attention on me and not Mico. "This isn't you."

The beast moves quickly in a threatening swipe of its my-face-sized paw. Prentis stands with the shadow creature, protecting the downed Nordeen. I risk a look over at Mico. He's done it right. The sea-drowned Africans' rage needed an outlet. Mico's banjo playing linked the old world with the new. They knew the sound of banjo, one of the few instrumentalities the Africans were able to retain through the middle passage. All of Mico's playing—the picking, slapping, the singing, even the harmonica playing—all of it with his right arm dominant, designed to wake the African spirits. They heard the songs of their children. Heard Mico's need, and like all good parents, they chose to fight for their child. His body is encased by a shifting black body armor. Black bodies big, otherworldly, strong. Strong enough to fend off the blows of Kothar.

My ankle goes red and white with soul pain. Not paying attention. The lion tagged my leg. Physical healing is irrelevant. The pain will stay. I jump back on my good leg and pull the entropy blades.

"Kid! You've got to fight him." I crouch low, beef up my calves, and let my eyes notice a larger stretch of the visual plane. I can see whatever liminal energy is building in the ghost lion, coursing through its body, prepping for another attack. "We can deal with these bastards with you on our side."

"You will die here, Taggert," Norden says for her, though he's still doubled in pain. I dodge a man-sized splinter broken by African-encrusted Mico over a pissed-off Kothar's head, only to catch the lion in mid attack.

I don't rise up but stay low, smelling the baked dirt. I curl into a ball as the lion rears up for me, then turn and kick up with enhanced legs at its chest. The blades work perfectly against my leg thrust as I hook its back paws as the lion sails skyward. It howls on its journey upward. Tamara flies directly into it, still reeling from some blow delivered from miles away. Not that it slows her down much.

"What the bloody hell?" she shouts, hovering over the juke joint's leaning frame. She holds the lion at bay with her power. Quickly she scans me.

"Bad kitty!" she yells and throws it down on top of Nordeen with the force of an asteroid. She rips half of Sally's sheet metal roof off and flees in pursuit of the Hookworm demon.

The lion drop caught Prentis off guard, so she feels the empathic brunt of it through the beast. Gives me a second to help Mico. By the steps, the Alter has his hands around Mico's throat. I run to one of the few cars left. Passenger side door is what's closest, so that's what I yank off. I throw it hard at the Alter's head. Nothing. Not even any indication he feels it as it skids through Sally's wall and floor. No choice. I've got to do it.

I will the entropy blades into my hands and jam them into Kothar's back. Nothing. Damn.

"Were you trying to get my attention, failed healer?" He's not stopping the choking. Over his shoulder I see Mico fighting for consciousness even through the armor of dead Africans. "Did you think your entropy butter knives would be any more than an annoyance to me? I am of the Black Liminal. The eternal spirit of my species. The perfect template. The sound of my native tongue drives your kind insane. I stand in contradiction to your reality. I defy any logic you can possibly master. And your best strike against me is two blades in the back?"

"I'm not trying to hurt you." This is going to hurt. "I'm going to heal you."

I fall into the abyss and am molested. The *fina materia* within him . . . it . . . them. I feel . . . absolute nothing. "I," as a term, becomes irrelevant because it indicates personhood. "A" being. There is nothing in this form. Not even form. It evaporates everything, this sensation. It erases all it touches, and when it's done, the sensation will evaporate itself. It's so much stronger in Kothar than Poppy. But soon even that separation is evaporated, as it, this great nothing, has been growing in me since I first felt Poppy. Before then. This is the truth that depression points to. Only this is no manufactured firing of neurons. This is the uncomfortable truth of the universe naked and felt. All things tend toward this stillness. Toward death.

It takes my fight first, the stillness. Then my mind. I beg for my eyes, to keep them open to look for hope, but I lose that petition as the stillness takes full control of my body.

But only for a second.

That which is liminal, whatever it is, cannot be still. It chatters like Prentis on a caffeine high; it scraps like Tamara when she's cranky. It sings like Samantha on a beautiful morning. It must move. My heart stopped—joining the entropy. But my liminality pulls it back. I had a heart attack, but with each new heartbeat I get stronger and reduce the power of the entropy. And Kothar. There's no way I'm in fighting shape, so I'm glad when Mico twists the Alter's hand off his throat and kicks him into the doorless car.

"You okay?"

"Pay attention!" I tell Mico, pointing to Nordeen behind him. My old teacher is up and pissed. That brain cancer is big and nasty in him but it's not slowing the bastard down.

Mico blacks up—angry arms, torsos, legs, and faces flickering in place of his—stomping toward Nordeen, when Poppy flies in from nowhere and shoves him into Big Sally's. Plywood, sheet rock, and glass give way like paper. Poppy flies around the porch, kicking every support beam down around the wrecked building. When the roof caves in I hear Mico scream from the inside.

"I've decided to rape your daughter for one hundred and fifty years. Do your kind live that long?" Poppy asks, juggling the beams in one hand as he levitates above me. He doesn't fly as much as give a "fuck you" to the laws of physics. Then to Nordeen, "Can you handle this?"

If I had any more energy, I'd be panicking right now. But I just had a heart attack. Poppy flies away, happy I'm about to die.

"Kid, I see you," I shout, getting up slowly. "Nordeen's got you all gothed out instead of your usual colors, but you can't help but have sleeve up, one sleeve down."

"Would that have mattered when you were mine, Taggert?" Nordeen hums as I walk toward him. Reduced as my power is, I see the liminal rising in Prentis. She's calling something.

"Once I knew what you were." Rubble is moving in what's left of Big Sally's. Good. Means Mico's not dead. That's a start. "Once I was clear you could never be trusted, that you would pervert and cheat and steal your advantage regardless of the cost to me—oh yeah, I prayed someone—anyone—would be able to see past what you made me do."

Around us, twelve Great Dane-sized husky hounds, made of the same dark dream material as the downed lion, all with red eyes, howl in unison. Johnson's fucking hellhounds.

"You should have prayed to a different god." Nordeen smiles. I pull my blades.

It's not even a word. A hymn grunt, and a strum. I've never heard him before today. I'll never forget that moanful sound. It's got that outsider logic, born from loss but programmed to endure. It harmonizes with intention, laughs and cries at the same long night. It's the will of life despite the certainty of death. It's the sound of the blues. As sung by Robert Fucking Johnson.

He plays off in the field, singing that damned song. Don't know what Mico was talking about. There is spirit in that song. The beasts turn toward his song in full attention. Then they take off at him, for prey or play, I can't tell, but the music doesn't die, it just fades away accompanied by the howls of the beasts. Guess Johnson learned to stop running for a second. I turn back to see a new sight in my old teacher's eyes. Caution.

"Touch me and I'll . . . ," he threatens but backs away as I sheathe my blades and walk toward Prentis. Struggling little Prentis.

"I'm not going to touch you. I'm going to heal her." Great thing about looking into the void named Kothar? Kind of cures you of any other fears. Like the fear of being controlled by Nordeen again if I attempted to heal Prentis. I felt her like an infection that I didn't want to catch on an unconscious level. No more. She's my girl.

"I told you, girl. You're with us now. You're never alone," I whisper into her ear and let whatever healing I have left pour into her. I don't have the strength to seal off her pain receptors. This is going to hurt. The both of us.

I'm in a fiery pain and half dead. But Prentis is in agony and fully aware. And pissed.

"You made me kill the animals!" she shouts at Nordeen, and I see real fear in him for the first time. Of course, it's from the vantage point of the ground. I can't stand.

"I unleashed the animal in you." Nordeen breathes hard, and white-hot sparks issue from his mouth.

"You turned predator into violator!" I've never seen Prentis this angry. And when she's angry, the animals around her get angry.

"I've shown you a world few can comprehend—"

"You took me from the only people that ever loved me. You abused me and the animals!" Ten times the number of rats that swarmed Big Sally's horde Nordeen. I hear a scream choked by a rat body, but that's just the beginning.

I didn't know how many owls there were in Mississippi until they all come to take bits of Nordeen. Then the bats. Then rattlesnakes. I knew about the coyotes. And of course the alligators, though I was surprised to see them come from the woods. Each take bits of Nordeen. Any attempt he makes to fight them off is stifled by a new attack. He doesn't stop screaming, even as three different 'gators go off with parts of him.

"Hey kid," I call out to Prentis from her feet.

"Taggert. You look like shit." There she is. The girl worth it all. Our heart. Our best part. Prentis.

"Been better, I won't lie. How about you?" She helps me stand.

"I'll never be okay again," she tries to joke. I take her face in my weak hands again.

"Yes, you fucking will." I hold her until she gets it. Or until Mico frees himself from Sally's rubble.

"Who's that?" she asks.

"Name's Mico."

"The DJ? Jah Puba?"

"Long story."

"When that guy punches you it's like all the bad things that ever happened to you happen again. Only you're the one doing the bad things," Mico informs us once he brushes half the building off himself.

"Hi, name's Prentis. I'm a fan. Legit like."

"Finally some recognition."

"Cut it—" Fucking rookies. I manage to push Prentis out of the way, but Kothar gets to pitch that doorless car right into Mico's chest. The whole pig-ironed car. Back into Big Sally's rubble pile he goes.

"Enough!" Kothar yells. "This distraction has already cost enough!"

"Agreed." Poppy descends from the sky with an unconscious Tamara suspended by her ponytail. He lands right next to Kothar. "This one is powerful, but sloppy."

"Tamara!" Prentis shouts. I want to as well, but it's like I'm having another heart attack. I thought—I knew—she could beat him.

"Idiots," Kothar scoffs at us. "Kill the girl and let's be done with it."

"What do you mean? She's already dead."

I love my sneaky little daughter. She masked her vitals, took a beating so she could get close. Close enough to get one in for Chabi. Take one to land five. The quick-movement Entropy of Bones technique. Not done as gracefully as Chabi, but with telekinetic aid it doesn't have to be. She manages to break chunks off of every one of his impossible bones.

"Psyche!" Tam grins, flying quickly over to our side. I pull blades, keeping an eye on Kothar as Poppy writhes in the ground in an agony even his worst enemies would pity. "We'll hug later, Prentis, yeah?"

"After we kick this wanker's head in?"

"Sure thing."

"You broke . . . who taught you how to break our bones?" Kothar hisses.

"A friend in a storm," she tells him. Kothar starts marching toward us, but a fridge in the face knocks him over. Mico. He clears himself once again from Big Sally's; awkward, but able. He's about to race forward to meet Kothar, but I stop him.

"Mico, you're not a fighter. Don't get mad. You're a singer. A unifier. It's not in your nature."

"I can do this!" he tells me.

"No. You can't. But they can," I tell him holding up his arm. "Give them your eyes and step out the way. Trust me."

Countless sets of African eyes flicker through his, taking the scene in. Big Sally's, Kothar, us. The tattoo surges. Outlines of radiant darkness—more suggestive of human form than representational—flow from Mico's arm and into direct combat with Kothar as he fights against Tamara's telekinetic push backwards. As they issue forth, Mico stops flicking, opting for a more direct combat.

Mico's not the best singer in the world. But when he does sing, or strum a banjo, or even DJ, he communicates clearly. He makes everyone feel like he's talking just to them. So he communicates our need, our want, our desperation to the Africans on his arm. Whatever ancient dark powers Kothar taps into, I don't think it can handle the collective suffering of the Middle Passage. They tear and break at Kothar, holding him, punching, infecting him. We stand back amazed and impressed. Until the tearing actually works.

All pretense of humanity ends when the Africans tear at Kothar's heart. What gives way isn't flesh and blood but a true vacuum, a hole in reality. A deep cold space refraction with a hunger for all matter and energy around us. Kothar is a human-sized black hole on Earth. Immediately half the number of spirits are sucked into it, but the remainder keep fighting. Big Sally's refuse, the car, stray rats—all of it gets sucked into this implacable void. We're next.

I stab into the ground with two hands as Mico and Prentis hold on to my body tight. Tam tries to stay aloft, but it's all she can do to push back against the vacuum. I can't . . . I can't reach her.

"You've already lost!" is the last thing I hear Kothar say. His legs then arms and head are sucked into his beating free space of a heart, along with more African spirits. But as he collapses on himself, the nothingness is sealed. The remaining spirits return to Mico's tattoo.

"Okay, I'll be needing that hug right now," Prentis says. Then she starts crying. Can't say I blame her.

Epilogue

The Unplanned Future

Kothar was right. The Manna was right. The wind boy was right. We were wrong.

Not that we knew it for the first three days after Kothar's void. Sally had converted a stable a few miles upcreek into a decent-sized five-bedroom spot for travelling musicians. She came running with her shotgun, danger be damned, when the death cries of her business shook the county. We were in such a state by the time she got to us, the woman felt she had to take us in. Johnson disappeared into the night to meet his fate in a few short months. Whether male Poppy was sucked into the void or crawled into some secluded blind with half his bones liquefied, he was gone before we left. Prentis took comfort in knowing Nordeen's face would never see daylight again. She'd been through enough. I'd tell her later that I've seen him come back from worse.

It took a full dreamless day for me to heal. Sally's oil-drum heater kept me warm. Her comforter-covered straw-from-the-field bed was surprisingly comfortable. The dream silence from Samantha was not. When I finally managed to blink my eyes awake it was an expectant Mico that stood guard over me.

"Touching the heart of an Alter is never a good idea," he told me, putting a curved green glass of milk in my hand.

"Haven't you heard? I'm filled with bad ideas." Through the second-story barn opening I saw Prentis walking the banks of the

157

creek with thousands of yellow, blue, and red butterflies behind her.

"You were right," Mico said, following my gaze. "She was worth it."

"I agree, but we still don't know the full cost." I told him about my Samantha dreams, including the last one. It was not shock or horror that grabbed his face. We'd been through too much for that. But it was close.

"But we won, right?"

"You asking or telling?"

"She told us to win. We did. Everything should be fine."

"Cool," I told him. "Then get us home."

He claimed it was a problem on his end. The African spirits were definitely an aid, but they were also a lot to carry. Without Chabi, who wasn't likely to come running, he'd have to negotiate the journey with them. He said it would take a few days. I didn't care.

It was like vacation for me and the girls. A secluded house by a river and woods filled with food for the smart and willing. Sally, being first and foremost a business woman, had done right and had her establishment insured as a "restaurant" by a black-owned bank in Harlem against "Acts of God." She told me if what hit the juke joint wasn't, she didn't know what was. She went North, claiming to be thankful she met us and in her words, "Prayerful that I never see y'all again."

Prentis and Tam sat and talked like sisters by the banks of the river for hours on end. Sometimes I heard tears, other times hysterical laughter. I gave them their space when I felt the need and went fishing. From across the banks I'd see them pointing at me sometimes.

"Yeah, we're talking about you, old man!" Tam would shout. Prentis sent butterflies and bunnies to keep me company. Our heart.

Mico spent all manner of hours doing his African spirit Tai Chi, trying to talk them into the journey. Without imminent threat of an Alter, the blood sacrifices of the juke joint or the hard-driving banjo guitar playing, they were proving a hard group to summon. Had I known what was waiting for us, I probably would've told him to stop trying so hard.

"I can't do it," he told us all over dinner one night. He didn't want to have to say it.

"Not enough juice?" Prentis's usual compassion was amplified a thousand times over when she heard what Mico gave up in order to come get her. She soothed his sadness with a gentle back rub.

"It's just . . . there's a block, something has changed . . . been . . ."

"Altered." Tam found the word for him. We all sat with the implication for a while. "No way in hell I'm staying in nineteen thirty whatever in the States, yeah? Shite, I thought '71 London was racist. Open your mouth around here and we're all liable to get lynched. 'Cept you, whitey," she joked at Prentis.

"Shut it, slag," Prentis quipped back. "Is there no one to call upon? To help?"

"The wind boy." In truth it was all I remembered. That nickname.

"He won't help," Mico came back.

"Who the bloody hell is the wind boy?" Tamara asked.

"I don't know, but . . . He was around, wasn't he?" I tried to pull the image into sight.

"He won't come," Mico protested. "His god won't let him."

"You turned on your god," Tam said harshly. "I'm sorry. I didn't mean to . . . Well, look, I'm just saying if this wind guy is your friend, yeah? Like for real and all. Well, you see what we just put on the line for a friend. Maybe he's, you know . . ."

"As nuts as us," I said. "Besides, it won't hurt to try, right?"

"Right, 'cause I swear if we're stuck in this time, we're moving to someplace that doesn't hate black people. Jaysis, you should hear this mental chatter. Makes me want to start a bloody racial war."

"I'll need your help," Mico finally consented. At the table we linked hands as Tamara projected the image of the wind boy into all our minds after she secured it from Mico. It was like seeing an old forgotten friend. Not someone dead, just forgotten. When we had the image fully rooted—his bandanna, his nutty little trench coat, his six-shooter, his entropy sword—Mico had us all say his name in unison: A.C.

The wind tore up our dinner table and sent everyone flying, but there he was. But what was once bright and light in him was haggard and bruised. Still, he gave everyone hugs. Even Prentis. When he got to me, I got a handshake like I'd done something important.

"I honestly didn't think you guys were going to make it," he told me.

"Don't feel bad, most people underestimate me and mine. Besides, I thought the Wind didn't want you associating with us types."

"None of that matters now. All the old truces and détente are over. There was a war. We lost."

A.C's ride back for us all wasn't as difficult as present-day London. Everything has . . . slipped. It's like that radiating cold from Kothar's heart infected the world. The entire globe. But its outward manifestation wasn't the Alter. It's Eel Pie Island under the benevolent control of my psychotic brother, Baron.

A.C. explained after he secured us in an abandoned movie theater in Brixton. It was all Mico could do to not shout from the rooftops as soon as he saw a dark brooding man on the telly screen, backed by an ultra high tech and modern hotel on his home island. It was the hot new story. Baron and his non-profit organization, The Amphictyony, was launching its latest venture to help the youth of the world by opening free health clinics for children throughout the U.K. and all its former colonies.

"You jumped in time," A.C. started, once we could all calm down. "So did they. At first I thought they were going for the Manna, but no. They were going for you, Mico. It's always been about you. I cut them off, with help, so many times. But they were relentless. They got an earlier version of you. Don't ask me which one. They replaced him—"

"With my brother." I hadn't told anyone initially. But A.C. knew. Tam almost choked. "How is my brother conscious, aware?"

"Because you weren't born." A.C. told me reluctantly.

"Fuck that, if he wasn't born, then . . ."

Tam's shock pulled me out of my own. "Easy, girl. You're here. You exist."

"The Alters have increased their power while radically reducing the Manna's," A.C. continues. "In our original time, the Alters already had control and predominance over finance and commerce as well as some cultural norms. But the underground—in terms of culture, psychology, aesthetics, even underground economies, Mico still had a chance to impact that kind of stuff. That's why the Manna made you link up with Fatima and Munji, see? But now the Alters exploit through explosion. Massive uncontrolled growth of everything is the new norm. That cool local cafe you loved? Well, now it's a multinational chain. The Oaxacan Mescal only made once a year that only select families knew about is now on the shelves at every major grocery outlet. Everything has been made unsustainably big and mass-marketed. They've made unlimited growth an agreed-upon goal for everything from ideas to weapons. The effect is subtle but incredibly destructive."

"Jaysis," Tam whispers after scanning the mind of the sea. "Everyone is exhausted, depressed. Fucking worse, it's normal for them. Everyone is just passively accepting it."

"The animals," Prentis almost cries, reclining in her movie seat. "It's wholesale massacre out there. Not just for food. They're killing everything."

"Music," Mico shouts. "The music has to reveal the truth. The real music has to be able to make people feel something, anything."

A.C. turns on a tube-amplified transistor and brings in pop pablum so bad even Prentis wouldn't dance to it. Then another station, and another. It's endless.

"Come on!" Tam snaps. "You're telling me all music sounds like this now? No one's singing with any soul?"

"Sure. Small pockets. But they know if they want to get recorded, get money, they have to convert to this soulless religion. The Manna held the heart aesthetic. Without its champion—"

"Manna would never allow this!" Mico shouts.

"The Manna didn't have a choice." A.C. can't help but sound accusatory. Very little of what they were saying mattered to me. I have one overriding concern.

"Where's Samantha?" Everyone goes silent.

"You're all going to want to sit down for this," the wind boy warns before calling up a video clip on a large desktop at the front of the theater. It's the grand opening of the Amphictyony, whatever the hell that is, on Eel Pie Island. The other Baron grins and waves to a crowd of people as excited as this version of reality tends to get. My brother—I've never seen him as an adult—suited in a $3000 get-up, is in his stride, at a podium about to make an announcement. Beside him, Samantha leans against the podium in a deep green dress looking gorgeously, sneeringly dangerous.

"No . . ." I hear my daughter cough. I swear I almost go hysterically blind. On the other side of the podium in a low-cut black evening dress, Yasmine, Tamara's mother, takes Baron's arm. Tam slams the computer into the back of the theater with her power. None of us move.

"How is my mom alive?" She stands.

"None of you are getting this. That's not your mother. She's a fire-starting Liminal under the Alter's sway. That woman never had a daughter. She never met Taggert. He doesn't exist in this timeline. That's the one thing you all have going for you in this era. None of you exist here."

"Bully for us," Prentis scoffs.

Mico gets up and walks away.

"This is all because you came for me?"

"Don't even think it," I tell Prentis.

"That it for you, then?" I ask Mico after a few hours. I find him in the projection booth laying on a discarded cot in the corner of the room, not a light on. I bring him the crap fast food A.C. pulled in for us. I guess flavor died in this time as well.

"Damn it, Taggert. Can you give me just a little time to grieve?"

"Screw you. The two loves of my life are hanging off of my brother's arm like a pair of matching bangles." I smile and offer him a burger.

"I can't. I can't even hear the Manna." He takes a bite reluctantly and is instantly regretful he did. "Everything is muted now."

"I know how important hearing is to you. And the Manna. We'll have to get them both back if we're going to fight this."

"What are you talking about? We did fight. On the wrong front. All your hitting in the face bullshit was . . . The Alters came up behind us and donkey-punched us right out of time!"

"And brought back some severe problems from the dead. Not to mention co-opting your friends and place of power. You left before A.C. showed us the Amphictyony website. Your little killers: I think Baron's turning them into his own personal army. Every kind act you did on that island Baron has twisted into something reprehensible."

"We lost!" he cries with tears larger than I've ever made.

"But we're still alive," I tell him softly. "You want me out of the game, you've got to kill me. I'm not dead. And I've got two knives designed to cut things that shouldn't exist. Like this entire fucking reality. Wind boy says he's down for the fight, so that's three sets of Entropy weapons down for the fight. Prentis is itching to avenge her animals and pay her debt to you. And you know Tamara loves a good scrap. Plus they resurrected her mom. Someone's got to pay for that."

"But without the Manna . . ."

"You've got countless angry African spirits that can tear apart an Alter living on your arm." He smiles a little. "I checked the footage. Ahmadi is with my brother. But there's no sign of Bingy or Narayana. Chabi's in the wind. No doubt she's dying to scrap with Alters again. And I bet that pilot girl might give you another shot now that you broke up with your god."

"Do you honestly think we can restore this world to sanity?"

"Was it sane before?" I laugh. "I don't know. Look, back when this all jumped off, you asked if we were friends. I judge my friends by their actions. And you, Mico L'Ouverture, are a bona fide action hero. You helped save Prentis. Now it's our turn to help you . . . and the world. I get your god now. It called me selfish because I was just thinking about what was important to me. Prentis. It was considering a larger world. I failed to see those implications, and, well, reality has paid the cost."

"And your response to that is to just as stubbornly fight to make things right now?"

"That's all we've got. You don't know my brother like I do. Nonprofit organization my ass. That dude is a bona fide psychopath. As a teen he pulled a house down on our heads. I am scared shitless of what he can do as a full-grown man. There's nothing that says we're going to win. Actually, everything indicates we are going to get our asses handed to us. As usual, we're outgunned and overwhelmed . . ."

"But we don't give up." He stands from the cot, his voice already more resonant.

"We never give up."

Acknowledgments

This is a story about doing what you think is right even when the world tells you its wrong. This is the story of my crew.

To D. Scott and Mave for taking me in, helping me out, cyphering and growing together.

To: Leigh and Michael: Because I know no better definition of family.

To Auntie Shukuru: Thank you for letting me always be me.
To Jesse Powell: For an editing eye.
To Natasha: For never giving up on us no matter what twists and turns we take. Forever my friend.
To Matty: For reaching out from the heart.

To Gavin and Kelly: For making this spectacle happen.

About the Author

Born in 1974, Ayize Jama-Everett hails from the Harlem of old. In his time on the planet, he's traveled extensively throughout the world—Malaysia, East and North Africa, Mexico, New Hampshire—before settling temporarily in Northern California. With Master's degrees in psychology and divinity, he's taught at the graduate and high school level and worked as a therapist. He is the author of three novels, *The Liminal People*, *The Liminal War*, and *The Entropy of Bones*, as well as an upcoming graphic novel with illustrator John Jennings entitled *Box of Bones*. When he's not writing, teaching, or sermonising, he's usually practicing his aim.

Read on for an excerpt from

THE ENTROPY OF BONES

by

AYIZE JAMA-EVERETT

Chapter One
The Time I Choked Out a Hillbilly

Last time I'd been this deep in the Northern California hills I was on a blood and bar tour in a monkey- shit brown Cutlass Royale with the Raj. Now I was on distance running from the Mansai, his boat, to wherever I would finally get tired. From Sausalito to Napa is only sixty or so miles if I hugged the San Pablo Bay, cut through the National Park, and ran parallel to the 121, straight north. About a half a day's run. Cut through the mountains and pick up the pace and I could make it to Calistoga in another three hours. From down-town wine country I'd find the nicest restaurant that would serve my sweaty gortexed ass and gorge myself on meals so large cooks would weep. The runs up were like moving landscape paintings done by masters, deep with nimbus clouds hiding in craggy sky-high moun-tains. Creeks hidden in deep green fern and ivies that spoke more than they ran.

Narayana Raj had taught me in the samurai style. You don't focus on your enemy's weakness; instead, you make yourself invulnerable. My focus was to be internal. In combat, discipline was all. But in the running of tens of miles, that discipline was frivolous. My only enemy was boredom and memory. Surrounded by such beauty, how could I not split my attention? Nestled in the California valleys, I found quiet, if not peace.

I also found guns. Halfway between Napa and Calistoga, the chambering of a shotgun pulled my attention from the drum and bass dirge pulsing in my ear buds. The woods had just gone dark, but my vision was clear enough to notice the discarded cigarette butts that formed a semicircle behind one knotted redwood. Rather than slowing down, I sped up and choke-held the red headed shotgun boy hiding behind the tree before he had time to situate himself, my ulna against his larynx, my palm against his carotid. He was muscular but untrained . Directly across from him was an older man, late thirties, dressed for warmth with one of those down jackets that barely made a sound when he moved. His almost fu-manchu mustache didn't twitch when he pulled two Berettas on me. I faced my captive toward his partner.

"Wait . . . ," Berettas said, more scared than he meant to sound.

Drop them. I commanded with my Voice. The gun went down hard. I used the Dragon claw, more a nerve slap than a punch, to turn the redhead's carotid artery into a vein for a second. When he started seizing, I dropped him. To his credit, Beretta went for the kid rather than his weapons. I continued my run, mad that I'd missed a refrain from Kruder and Dorfmeister.

As an indication of where my head was, I confess to not thinking about the scrap until a week later. Finishing the run, swimming ten miles a day, keeping the *Mansai* in shape, and avoiding my mother at the other end of the pier as much as possible, covered the in-between time. Even when I went back up the same route for my big run, the redhead was an afterthought.

It was only when I hit Calistoga, almost desperate for my calorie load for the run back to the Bay, that I had to deal with the consequences of my choke-hold. I liked hitting up the nice tourist joint restaurants for grub when I was sweaty, and paying cash for double entrée meals. The place smelled of wood and fire, but most of the fixtures were constructed out of industrial iron and brass. Servers dressed in white shirts and black slacks prayed the heavy-fingered piano player's jazz standards would cover the clang of their dropping silverware on the brass tables. Most patrons came in dressed in custom suits and designer dresses. Me, I've always been sweats 'n' hoodies girl. Usually I was the most out-of-place-looking person in the spot. But not that day.

I was devouring two orders of BBQ oysters, fries and half a broiled chicken when a bear-looking man walked in. Seriously, he was 6'9", three hundred pounds of muscle with another twenty-five pounds of fat for padding. He was local. I'd seen skinnier versions of his face in the area, long in the cheekbones, bullet marks where eyes should be. He wore a large red flannel shirt and Carhartts fit for a bear. But what stood out was his facial hair. It made a mockery of any other beard I'd ever seen. His hair started on his head and covered every part of his face, from pretty close to his eye sockets to well past his collar line. It seemed almost bizarre that a mouth existed under all that fur. But it made him easy to read. As soon as he saw me, the hair moved into a smile. All the wait staff and bartenders seemed to know him. It wasn't until he sat at my table facing me that I saw any relation to the red-head in the woods. I'm not usually one for weapons, but I palmed my butterfly knife on the off chance the bear tried to maul me in public.

"What do you weigh in at? One hundred and twenty pounds? Sopping wet?" he asked after it became obvious I wasn't going to stop eating.

And you care because?

"I'm just wondering where all that food goes," he said with a laugh. "What? You one of those bulimics or something?"

Mind not talking about gross shit while I'm eating? I snapped.

"Apologies. Didn't realize you were so sensitive."

The waitress delivered a slice of key lime pie and a glass of red wine so casually I knew she'd supplied the same to him dozens of times before.

That's going straight to your hips, I said while shoving a handful of fries in my mouth. He laughed for a while before he could take a bite of pie.

"I knew this teacher, Filipino chick or something. One of those goody-goodies. Worked at a private school in Frisco. Coached soccer, taught all day, would drive up here and take dirt samples all around my vineyard, acres and acres. All for her thesis. She never broke a sweat." He looked at me like I was supposed to get it. I kept eating.

"Turned out she had this hyperthyroid condition. Made her super strong, super fast, sped up her metabolism something fierce . . . "

Like a superhero, I said laughing and chewing my chicken.

"Exactly," the bear growled back. "Only if she hadn't have gotten it fixed, it would have killed her."

Believe me I was listening for the threat. I stopped eating and stared the bear down. To his credit, he didn't blink. But he didn't keep eating either.

I get the sense you're trying to tell me something, I said after I pulled my arms under the table.

"Then you misconstrue me entirely young lady. I'm filled with nothing but questions."

Better you ask straight away then.

"Was that you that choked out my nephew, not nine miles from here while his uncle stood by and watched?"

Your nephew the sort to chamber a pump action on a jogger while she's minding her own damn business?

"It took him two days to fully recover."

But he recovered. I leaned back in my chair, spinning my knife to my wrist, ready for whatever came next. The waitress poured another glass of Syrah.

"My brother, the one with the moustache, said he'd never seen anybody adjust to a threat as quick as you did." I nodded. "He's been in Kosovo, Iraq, Afghanistan. But you impressed him. My nephew took a different path. Did six years in Angola, the prison, you understand, not the country. Another three in San Quentin before he got smart about his game. You got the drop on him, and he saw you coming. Now you eat like a horse, but aside from that you don't say much, seem tough as nails and can obviously handle yourself. Type of business I'm in, I can't help but ask if you're looking for work."

First time I met Narayana the entire pier was being threatened by snakes. Some idiot independent filmmaker decided he wanted to make a sequel of a movie that he didn't own the rights to. He was shooting it "guerilla style," meaning without a script, a proper crew, or a clue. Oh yeah, and it involved snakes on a boat. The majority of houseboats on our Sausalito pier were like the one I grew up in, more house than boat. You'd have better luck finding alcoholics and '80s radicals living off the grid in those forever moored houses than a sailor or anyone with a hint of grit in them. So when the pock-faced 20-something filmmaker's snakes escaped after a drunken wrap party, let's just say things got chaotic.

Screams of panic didn't rouse my mom from her drunken snoring back then. But I got curious. Not yet fully dark and all I could see were squirming shadows darting to and fro on the dock, in the bushes, out of people's boats, falling in the water. Some of the snakes were thinner than a pencil and lightning quick; some moved so heavily across the port they seemed to dare you to touch them. Folks were grabbing their children and pets and locking themselves in their boats or trying to run past the snakes to get off the pier. I turned to go back inside when a coil hissed at me.

It was a hooded cobra. Don't ask what kind, I wouldn't be able to tell you. I just know it was banded, tan, and hissing. It stood between me and the walkway that went down to my boat house. I tried backing up but in doing so I dragged my foot, a sound which agitated the snake. It raised its head a little more and hissed in a lower tone than I thought it would. What freaked me out more was that I thought I heard my name in its hiss.

I didn't have time to focus on it. From behind me, a man five inches shorter than me and two shades darker appeared. His arms were so muscular and veiny they looked like a knot of rebar. But they were as skinny as his legs. What little hair he had was a deep red and mostly near his temples. He wore an Ice Cube Predator shirt and carried a large metal trashcan. I couldn't figure out which one I should be more cautious of: the snake or the man. He didn't give me a choice.

"Hold this," Narayana told me as he took the lid and handed me the can. With circular steps that never left the dock, the tiny man pushed lesser snakes out of his way with his foot until he was able to squat in arm's length of the coiled cobra. What noise, cold, and chaos had been all around disappeared in the distance as I watched this stranger speak in angered tones to this snake in a language I almost understood. After a while, he seemed to get frustrated. So he slapped the snake. Hard. The snake hissed lower, I swear almost speaking. He slapped it again. It opened its mouth in time with the tides, methodically quickly.

Again, Narayana slapped its head. I didn't see it strike. I didn't see it move. But Narayana did. Faster than a bullet he raised the trash lid. The snake's mouth made a harsh thud against it, but before it could fall to the deck, Narayana grabbed its head with his other hand. He stood with it as the snake's body, more than double his length, flopped and fought. But it was useless; his rebar hands would not let go. He held it close to his face, staring in its eyes, and spoke to it in a thick accent.

"I'm free. Tell your masters." He threw it hard in the trashcan and slammed the lid on top. If he noticed me, he didn't say anything as he grabbed the can from my hands. But I couldn't forget him. Not ever.